The Jungle Inside

The Jungle Inside

Avril Sabine

Cracked Acorn Productions
Australia

The Jungle Inside

Published by

Cracked Acorn Productions

PO Box 1365

Gympie, Queensland 4570

Australia

978-1-925131-14-7 (Kindle)

978-1-925617-29-0 (EPUB)

978-1-925131-27-7 (Print)

Genre: Young Adult Urban Fantasy

Copyright 2014 © Avril Sabine

Cover design by Caitlyn Petersen

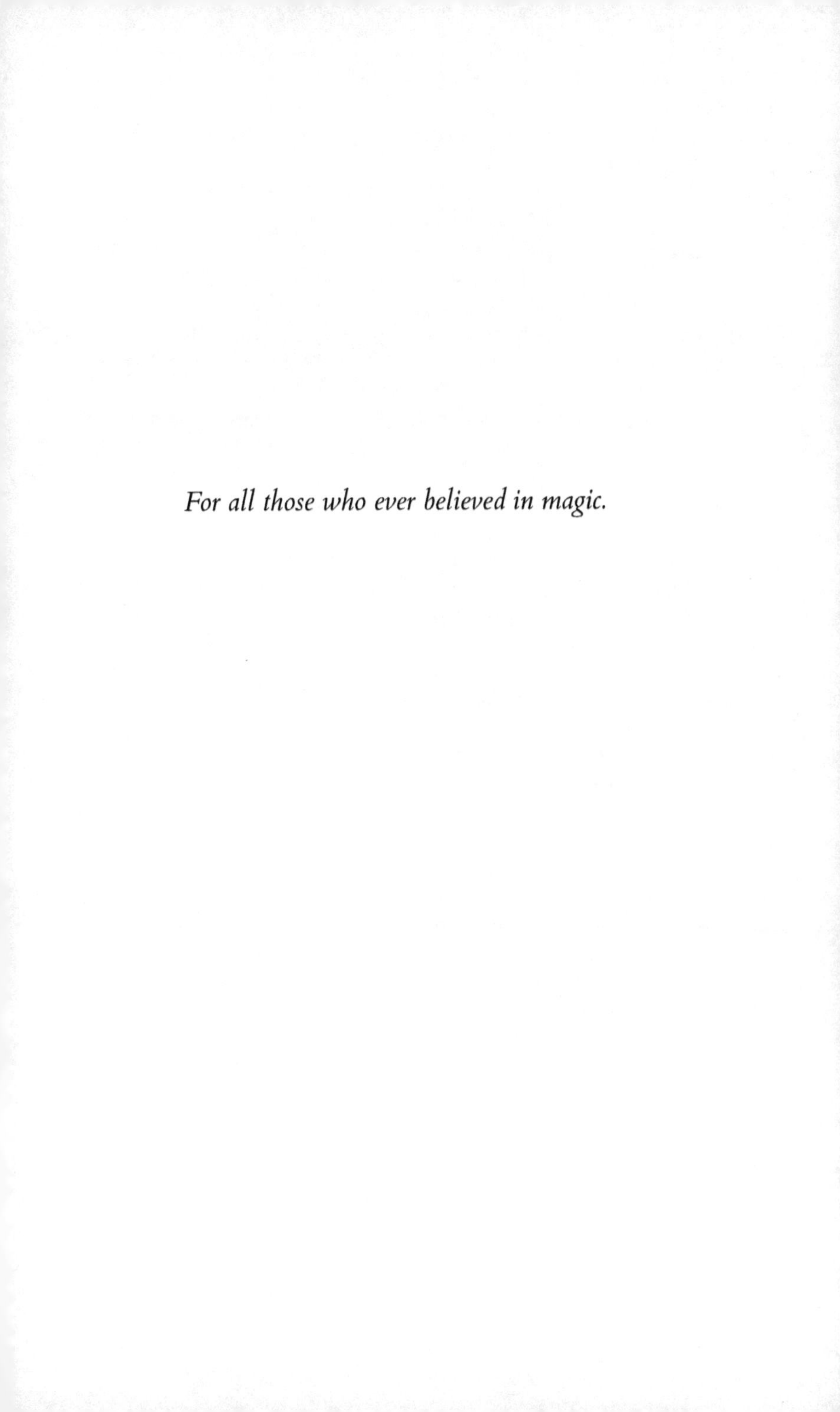

For all those who ever believed in magic.

All Eden wanted was one normal weekend. She finally had a friend who knew nothing about her family. A friend who didn't believe the rumours, because witches didn't exist. But as usual, nothing was going according to plan. Her mother had promised no magic while Tory was visiting, but she couldn't help doing one simple spell before Tory arrived. It was a pity there was nothing simple about the results.

*

This story was written by an Australian author using Australian spelling.

Chapter One

Eden groaned when she opened her eyes. Strands of vines still crept in around the frame of her closed bedroom door. Groaning again, she rolled over and buried her head under her pillow. It didn't help. She could still see them clearly in her mind. Dark green tendrils creeping through the edge of the door and across the white of the doorframe as they reached out to the cream coloured walls. She flipped back over and threw her pillow at the door. The dull thud caused something to screech on the other side. Eden rolled out of bed, keeping her gaze on the door. When no other sounds filtered through she moved towards her duchess.

"No wonder I never have friends over." Again her gaze was drawn to the door. Why couldn't she have a normal mother who did normal things like, she stopped mid thought as she tried to come up with something normal. What did she know about normal? Obviously nothing.

She grabbed the brush off her duchess and ran it through her short, sandy brown hair. After sliding in a couple of clips to hold it out of her green eyes, she rummaged through the clothes on the floor of her wardrobe. She gave the t-shirt and skirt of her school uniform a shake before she changed into them. Pausing at her bedroom door, Eden took a deep breath. It was quiet on the other side, but she remained in place. Last night she'd learned that quiet wasn't always good, but that didn't mean it was bad either. She couldn't stand here all day or she'd be late to school. Her stomach rumbled. Besides, she was hungry and wanted breakfast.

Picking up her schoolbag, she slung it over one shoulder and took hold of the stout stick that leaned against the wall. Opening the door slightly, she peered into the hall.

Where there had once been faded, floral carpet there were now leaves and vines. Only the odd patch of the carpet showed through. Most of the walls were hidden by vines and in some places large tree trunks seemed to grow out of them, roots snaking across the hidden carpet. Colourful birds and monkeys moved about in the thick vegetation and unseen creatures scampered through the undergrowth. But it was all strangely quiet. The birds no longer sang and the monkeys had ceased their chatter.

Eden froze in the doorway. Wasn't silence in the jungle usually a warning? She glanced around the narrow hallway, made even narrower by the vegetation. Everything seemed safe. Maybe it was her they were afraid of. She gripped her stick tighter. Standing around staring was not getting her anywhere.

Eden slipped into the hall, closing her bedroom door behind her. "She promised to get rid of it. She always promises. But does she ever do what she promises?" Shaking her head, she hurried along the hall, swinging her stick to break the vines that blocked her way. The same action she'd been forced to use to find her bedroom last night. She stopped in front of the bathroom door and had to pull vines away from the doorknob before she could open it.

"It's always the same," Eden muttered. "You think she'd learn by now. It never, ever, ever–" Eden screamed, slamming the bathroom door shut. Her breath came quickly as she backed away, stopped from retreating further by the wall facing the bathroom door. Around her monkeys screeched and birds squawked as if they'd also seen inside the bathroom. "No. Oh, please no," she whispered as silence returned to the hall. "I'm imagining things. I have to be imagining things. The monkeys and parrots I can handle. Even the creepy things that never show themselves. But this, this is too much. Maybe it was just my imagination."

Hesitantly Eden stepped forward, her hand outstretched. Just as she touched the bathroom doorknob, shrieks down the hall made her scream again and jump back, her hand pressed against her racing heart. "It was a monkey. Only a monkey." She looked up the hallway, but her gaze was soon drawn back to the bathroom door. "Come on. Just open the door." Eden groaned and closed her eyes. "Great. Now I'm talking to myself. I never talk to myself. Mutter occasionally, but never talk to myself. What can I expect? It's crazy here. Of course I'm going insane. Only sixteen-years-old and they're going to cart me away and lock me up with all the other completely insane people." Her fingers tightened on the stick. "This is crazy. Completely and utterly crazy."

Taking a deep breath and straightening her back, Eden stepped forward, opening the door. Her mouth dropped open and she stared at the tiger crouched on the bathroom mat. There was a low rumble and then the tiger's muscles bunched like it was going to jump. With a scream, Eden slammed the bathroom door shut. There was a thud and the door shook. Eden's breath shuddered out as she backed into the wall.

"That's it. I've had enough." Forcing shaky limbs to work, she stormed along the hall and down the stairs, swinging her stick as she made her way through the lush growth. Startled monkeys shrieked at her and parrots flew away, loudly voicing their annoyance at being disturbed. "Don't talk to me like that." Eden pointed an accusing finger at one of the monkeys. "I belong here. You don't." Fighting her way through the jungle, Eden finally made it to the kitchen, dropping her schoolbag on the floor. "Mum!"

Opal Merrett looked up from the large, old, leather bound book she flicked through. "Good morning, love. Sleep well?"

Chapter Two

Eden glared at her mother. "You promised. You said you'd do no more magic in the house. Then you promised you'd deal with this mess. Have you forgotten it's Friday?"

"But it was dying." Opal waved her hand towards the small African violet sitting in a pot on the kitchen table. Purple flowers were surrounded by lush green leaves. "How could I tell Aunt Edith I'd let it die?"

"You could have bought another one and told her it was the one she'd given you."

"She'd know."

"So what?" Aunt Edith was her grandmother's busybody older sister. Older than her by ten years. "She'd get over it. But what about me? You promised we could have my best friend and her brother here for the weekend. You promised. Just like you promised no more magic. You can't do it. And I don't care how good Grandma and Grandad were. You. Just. Can. Not. Do. Magic!" Eden grabbed the back of one of the kitchen chairs, trying to calm down. It was impossible. The entire situation was impossible.

"I wouldn't yell like that dear. There's something sleeping in the pantry. We wouldn't want to disturb it." Opal turned another page, ran her finger down the words, shook her head and turned several more pages.

"Mum!"

"I know, I know. But I was sure I'd be able to do that spell. It is such a simple one. Why, my mother used to be able to do spells like that in her sleep. I didn't mean for it to get out of hand like it did. I'm sure I'll have it all under control by this afternoon." Opal tucked a strand of her light brown hair, which had escaped from her braid, behind her ear. "But, just in case, you might want to take your friends to the downstairs room this afternoon. The jungle doesn't seem to have reached there yet."

"And tell them what? We've got to spend the weekend down here. There's a bathroom and TV, what more could you want? Oh, no, sorry. Can't show you my room. No, you'll have to wait here while I bring you food. And sorry about this bathroom. I know the water pressure is shocking and the toilet makes a dreadful noise when you flush, but it is an old house after all. And yes, we do have another bathroom." Eden's voice continued to rise. "But you can't use it because there's a tiger in there."

Opal looked up from the book. "Really? Is that the upstairs or downstairs one?"

"What does it matter? The whole point is that we have a tiger in our house. No one. And I mean no one has to put up with the rubbish I do. You'd think after that stupid birthday party, where you tried to get stars to float above us and some of the kids were burned by the exploding stars, you'd know you weren't meant to do magic."

Opal waved a hand airily. "Oh, that was so long ago. I would have thought you'd have forgotten it by now."

"I was three-years-old and most of those kids are still at my school and have scars from my party. At least they only thought you were trying to set off fireworks in the house. I can't imagine what they would've said if they'd known the truth. Now, stop trying to make me lose track of what I was saying." Eden glared at her mother, her fingers tightening on the back of the chair until her knuckles were white.

"What were you saying, love?" Opal turned another page in her book. "I know the counter spell must be in here somewhere. I just hope it doesn't reverse what I did for the violet. Aunt Edith will be really upset if I let it die. I can just imagine what she'll say." Her large blue eyes blinked rapidly as if she fought to hold back tears.

Eden's anger died as she crossed the room to place a hand on her mother's arm. "Who cares about Aunt Edith? She's a bitter old bat who doesn't know what she's talking about. Grandma and Grandad were never disappointed in you. They didn't care that you can't do magic, or that I can't either." Ever since her grandparents had died Aunt Edith had been trying to take their place and doing a terrible job of it. All she did was complain and point out their faults and what a disappointment the two of them were to the family. The last of a noble and powerful line and they couldn't do an ounce of magic between them.

"You're a sweetheart, Eden. I don't know what I'd do without you." Opal placed her hand over Eden's.

"Yeah, well how about you remember that and try and do something about this mess. Now, I'd better have breakfast or I'll be late for school." Eden strode towards the pantry, completely forgetting her mother's earlier warning. "Mum!" Eden shrieked as she opened the pantry door. She slammed it shut. "There's a thirty metre long snake in there."

"What dear?" Opal looked up from her book.

"Snake. Thirty metres long. Pantry." Eden glared at her mother, hands on her hips, her earlier sympathy gone.

"I did tell you it was in there and thirty metres is a bit of an exaggeration. I'm sure they don't grow that long. It probably looks bigger because of how small our pantry is."

"Mum! What about breakfast? I'm starving. I couldn't brush my teeth because of a tiger and now I can't eat breakfast because of a snake that could probably wrap itself around our house twice."

"You really shouldn't exaggerate so much, Eden. Remember the story about the boy who cried wolf?"

Right now she didn't care about some old tale. She was hungry. "Breakfast?"

"Oh, right. Grab some money out of my bag." Opal shook her head. "I can't understand why I haven't found the spell yet." She turned another page then glanced at Eden. "Get something to eat on the way to school."

Eden stared at her mother as she frowned over yet another page. Why couldn't she manage one weekend of normal? Was that too much to ask? Just one weekend. She sighed. "I need enough money for a new toothbrush and toothpaste. There's no way I'm going in that bathroom until the tiger's gone. And I mean back to where he came from, not out of the bathroom and wandering around the house," Eden said.

Opal continued to run her finger down the page in front of her. "Okay."

"Can you get me some gear together for tonight? Sleeping bags, clothes, junk food and whatever else I might need. I won't have time now or I'll be late to school. I didn't think I'd need to relocate before school this morning."

"Sure, love," Opal said absently as she continued to flick through her book.

Eden sighed, hoping her mother had paid attention to what she'd said. "See you, Mum."

"Okay, love." She stopped turning pages. "Hmm, this looks interesting."

Eden's gaze remained on her mother for another minute. No wonder she didn't have a clue what normal was. Grabbing her schoolbag, she headed for her mother's handbag. If she was lucky, the jungle would be gone by afternoon. A monkey screeched at her as she passed it. Eden glared at it. She didn't like her chances.

Chapter Three

"Mum! I'm home." As Eden approached the back door she was tempted to cross her fingers. She glanced over her shoulder at the two dark haired, dark eyed teenagers that followed her. The girl looked around with interest, while the boy glared at his surroundings. Both, like her, were wearing their school uniforms. Eden breathed a sigh of relief when her mother came out the back door. She didn't have to think of an excuse about why she couldn't take her companions inside with her.

"Hello, love. How was your day?" Opal smiled at Eden, her smile widening as she glanced at her daughter's companions.

"All right," Eden said cautiously. "How's everything?"

"Same as this morning," Opal said. "Are you going to introduce me to your friends?"

Eden bit back the angry words she knew her friends wouldn't understand, trying to remain calm. This weekend had to go well. It just had to. "This is Victoria Davenport. She's in my class. Everyone calls her Tory. And this is her brother Heath. He's a grade above us."

"Hi, Mrs Merrett. Thanks for having us this weekend," Tory said.

"Oh, call me Opal. I don't know if Eden told you, but I thought you might like to stay in the rumpus room this weekend. I'm sure you won't want me in the way. Now if you wait a minute, I'll bring out some afternoon tea for you to take with you." Opal disappeared inside.

Eden felt slightly hopeful. So far everything was going okay. Except for Heath, but she couldn't really blame him. What seventeen-year-old boy wanted to hang out with their sister for the weekend?

Tory elbowed her brother who continued to frown. "You could have at least said hello. It's not our fault Mum and Dad are treating you like a little kid and won't let you stay at home while they're away. You're the one who ruined it for yourself with that party when they went away to celebrate their twentieth wedding anniversary. You've only got yourself to blame."

Eden started to speak, not wanting an argument to start, but Heath spoke before she had the chance.

"I can't believe they let us come here when everyone knows her mother's crazy."

Eden stared at him, her mouth opening, only to close, words unspoken. She tried not to let it bother her. Tried to tell herself he wasn't really angry at her. But she didn't believe herself. He wasn't the first who'd spoken those words.

"That was mean, Heath. Sometimes I can't believe you're my brother. And besides, you can't talk. If you had any friends, you could have stayed with them," Tory said.

"I've got friends. They were all busy. It's not like Mum and Dad gave anyone much notice. Two days notice isn't enough for anyone," Heath growled.

"Like Grandma could have planned her emergency surgery ahead of time. You're so stupid sometimes," Tory hissed.

"At least I don't have the school reject for my best friend," Heath muttered.

Eden took a step back, as if hit. Her hands curled into fists and she fought the urge to strike out at him. To hurt him as much as he was hurting her.

"You take that back, Heath." Tory's eyes widened. "I can't believe you said that."

"Can't you handle the truth? This weekend will suck." Heath turned away, striding into the backyard that was full of shady trees and shrubs that had run wild. "Don't you believe in doing the gardening?" He threw the words over his shoulder before he stepped into the shadows created by the trees.

Before Eden had a chance to defend their yard, Opal came out the back door. She had a plate with biscuits, patty cakes and chips in one hand and a jug of fruit juice in the other. A stack of cups were held between her arm and waist. "Grab the juice, Eden. I don't want to drop it."

Eden took the juice and cups while Tory reached for the plate. "Thanks, Mrs Merrett."

"Have fun." Opal started to go inside and then stopped, looking around. "What happened to Heath?"

"He went for a walk." Eden tried not to think about what he'd said. He could spend the weekend in the backyard for all she cared. The less she had to see him the better.

"Ah, that might not be the best idea." Opal moved forward several steps. "Heath. Heath!"

"Yeah?" Heath stepped out of the trees.

"You might not want to wander around the yard,

particularly when it gets dark. We've got a bit of an animal problem," Opal said.

Animal problem? Eden had a sinking feeling.

"I'll be all right." Heath folded his arms across his chest, transferring most of his weight to his left leg.

"Ah, well, the neighbour's dog got loose again and he's rather… er… unfriendly." Opal glanced around the yard.

The sinking feeling increased. Eden's eyes narrowed. "Neighbour's dog?"

"Yeah, you know. Tiger." Opal stared at Eden.

"Mum." Eden groaned and her eyes momentarily closed. This wasn't happening. And here she'd thought the afternoon wasn't going too bad. Apart from Heath that was.

"It's not like your mother can control your neighbour's dog," Tory said.

Eden clenched her teeth together, counting to ten. It didn't help. Maybe counting to a million might. "Come on. Let's go downstairs before the dog," she shot a look towards her mother, "finds us out here."

"It should be okay while it's daylight," Opal said. "And as long as you stay out of the trees. I'll ahh… leave you to it." She slipped back inside.

Eden stared after her mother. Typical. Make a mess

then expect everyone to shrug it off like it was no big deal.

Heath crossed the open part of the yard, stopping beside Eden. "What sort of dog is he?"

Eden shrugged, walking towards the rumpus room door. "I don't know, a bit of a mixed breed I guess. But he's as big as a tiger and has the attitude of one." She opened the rumpus room door. It had once been a garage, built underneath one side of the house where the land sloped away. Striding into the dimly lit interior, she put the jug and cups on a coffee table. "Can you get that switch?" She nodded towards it.

Tory, still in the doorway, turned on the light. "Oh, you're so lucky. This place is great." She closed the door once her brother entered the room.

"Hmph," Heath grunted as he passed the table just inside the door, ignored the pool table and dropped onto one of the lounge chairs placed in front of the television. "How old does your mum think we are?" He propped his feet on the coffee table.

"Get your feet off there." Tory pushed her brother's feet onto the floor so she could put the plate down.

"Well, look at it. She might as well have given us milk and cookies." Heath gestured towards the plate.

"That's it. I don't care how many times you pay out on me at school with all your mates and those other idiots in my class, but you will not run my Mum down in our own house." Eden glared down at him, hands on her hips, her lips pressed tight together.

Heath smiled slightly. "Back off. If you can't handle the truth that's your problem."

Anger flooded Eden, bringing with it flashes of images. "You want to know what the truth is?" She leaned closer, jabbing a finger at his chest, the images becoming stronger. "You think you've got to act tough because you don't want to be as friendless in this town as you were in your last one. That you aren't going to do well at school and even look at a computer because you don't want to be called a freak again for knowing everything."

Heath leapt to his feet, pushing Eden from him as he turned on his sister. "You told her. You promised not to tell."

Chapter Four

Eden shrieked covering her mouth with her hand, her eyes wide. What had she done? She sank into the nearest chair, pulling her legs up to wrap her arms around them. "No, no, no. Oh please no."

Tory looked wildly between her angry brother and her moaning friend. "I didn't tell her anything. I don't know how she knew. Anyway, you deserved it. You've been nasty ever since we got here. No. Even before we got here. And you've got no one to blame but yourself for being here. You were the idiot who threw a party last time we had the house to ourselves."

"You had to tell her. How else could she know? Are you trying to tell me she can read minds?" Heath demanded.

Eden groaned when Tory and Heath turned to look at her. "I think I'm going to be sick." She ran outside, her hand clamped over her mouth, glancing around. There was no way she was going to throw up in the yard with a tiger on the loose. Running into the kitchen, she stopped when she saw her mother at the stove stirring a noxious smelling liquid. She froze, not knowing what to say or do. She felt sick to her stomach. There was no way she wanted to be able to read thoughts or do magic of any description. It wrecked your life.

Opal looked over at Eden and dropped the spoon, rushing to Eden's side. "What's wrong, love? Is everything all right? The tiger didn't get one of your friends did he? I don't know how we'd explain that. I just can't imagine."

Eden shook her head, unable to speak. She could only think about the words she'd said in her anger. Words that had seemed to pour into her head and straight out her mouth. They had come from nowhere.

"Baby, you've got to tell me what's wrong. I can't read minds you know."

Eden moaned, shuddering at the thought of reading minds. "Tell me about..." Eden began and then stopped.

"What, love?" Opal wrapped her arms around Eden.

"When I was little. When the magic went really wrong. When you knew I couldn't do it."

"Oh, that was so long ago. You were helping me with one of my spells and I let you finish it off and there was such an explosion we thought the house might blow up. We all thought it might have been my fault so your father insisted we let you try again. I supervised of course. You were too little to be let loose with magic. That explosion was just as bad as the first one. The neighbours even called the police and they wanted to look around. I'll never forget that day. Your father told them we thought the noise had come from the neighbour's house. Everyone was baffled for months. And the Watkins family hasn't talked to us ever since."

"So I can't do magic, right?" Eden asked.

"What happened?" Opal asked.

Eden hesitated, but keeping quiet wouldn't make it any less real. She told her mother about knowing Heath's secrets.

Opal grinned, squealing in excitement. "Maybe you're a late developer."

"I don't want to be able to do magic. It's nothing but trouble." Eden gestured towards the kitchen that was half jungle.

"Eden!" Tory called from outside.

"I've got to go. I can't let her in here." Eden pulled away from her mother and rushed for the back door. "They can't know we can do magic. This is the first friend I've had in years. Every time I've made a friend, they've been scared off by all the weirdness in our family."

Opal continued to smile. "We'll talk about this after the weekend."

"It's not good news," Eden muttered.

"I guess it depends on your perspective."

Tory banged on the back door. "Eden."

"I'm here." Eden slipped outside, careful not to open the door very far.

"Are you all right?" Tory asked. "I'm sorry about my brother. He's a complete idiot sometimes."

"I can do my own apologising." Heath stepped out from amongst the trees, the shirt of his school uniform smudged by dirt on one sleeve.

"You'd probably make a mess of it," Tory said. "For a so called genius you can be such an idiot."

"I'm sorry." Heath came closer. "After all the tormenting I've copped you'd think I'd know better. I didn't mean any of it. So what if your mum's a little weird? I've spent all my life being called weird. Which means it can't be that bad a thing to be."

Heath grinned for the first time that afternoon. "I shouldn't have taken my bad mood out on you."

Eden tried to hold onto her anger. "I don't-"

"Heath," Tory hissed. "Heath! Look." Tory's left hand covered her mouth while her other hand shakily pointed to Heath's right.

Eden's gaze followed the direction. "Heath. Run!" She turned, opened the kitchen door and shoved Tory inside before she faced Heath.

After a startled look to where his sister had pointed, Heath ran for the back door. The tiger that had crept closer to Heath sprang forward when he saw his prey about to escape. The pounding of Heath's feet was drowned by the sound of the tiger's snarl.

"Run," Eden screamed as the tiger sprang. She automatically stepped forward, right hand held up, and shouted, "No!" The tiger bounced backwards, like it had hit a brick wall, instead of landing on Heath who had only been a paw's length away. Eden stared at the tiger as he picked himself up, shook and snarled angrily. He gathered himself together and ran forward again. Shocked, Eden could only stare as the tiger came closer. The powerful muscles moved under his fur as his long stride quickly covered the ground.

"Eden." Heath grabbed her by the arm and dragged

her into the kitchen, slamming the door shut. There was a thud against the door and claws raked the timber, followed by an angry snarl.

Eden continued to stare at the door. This was a nightmare. A complete and utter nightmare. She slowly turned, checking that everything was still the same. It was. Nothing had changed and now Tory and Heath were about to find out exactly how weird her mother was.

"What is going on around here?" Heath looked at the kitchen, the jungle forcing its way out of the walls, leaves littering the floor.

"Welcome to my life." Eden leaned against the wall near the door.

"How did this get here?" Heath asked. "It's amazing. Are these trees growing out of the walls or have the walls been built around the trees?" He moved to the closest wall so he could examine the tree trunk. "Amazing."

With an apologetic look towards Eden and a shrug, Opal answered. "Magic. The trees are growing out of the wall."

"It doesn't look like an illusion." Heath touched the tree trunk tentatively.

"Great." Tory finally found her voice. "The first thing you show interest in after being in this town for three months has to be even weirder than you. Hello? Doesn't anyone realise there's a tiger out there? And what do you mean magic? There's no such thing."

"I know what it's all about. They film movies here, don't they?" Heath grinned. "I knew there'd have to be a logical explanation. Where are the animal handlers? Will the film crew be here over the weekend? Do you think they'll let me check out some of their equipment? Is the rest of the house like this?"

"Considering you didn't even know how to say hello, when you first arrived, you've certainly got a lot to ask now," Opal said.

"Sorry," Heath said. "I thought this weekend would be a bore. How many guys do you know that want to hang around with their kid sister? Can I look around?"

Opal shrugged. "Be my guest." She waved towards the hallway entrance. "Oh, and avoid the lounge room. There were strange noises in there earlier."

"What sort of strange noises?" Eden asked suspiciously.

"You know," Opal shrugged, "the strange sort."

"Great. Something else to worry about," Eden muttered.

"Is this really a movie set?" Tory asked. "Can I have a look around too?"

"Why don't you two go ahead and Eden will join you in a minute?" Opal suggested.

As soon as they were alone in the kitchen, Eden asked, "So what's in the lounge room?"

Chapter Five

Opal shrugged. "I wouldn't have a clue what's in the lounge room. That wasn't what I wanted to talk to you about. I think I've figured out how to reverse the spell, but I'm afraid I won't be able to save the violet." She looked regretfully towards the table. The violet had grown more leaves and flowers since that morning.

Eden barely spared it a glance. "Who cares about the violet? What about the tiger outside that tried to eat us? You have to get rid of all this, now." She gestured towards the walls.

"Yes, of course, but what about your friends? We won't be able to hide the fact it's magic. How do you think they'll take it? Do you think we should wait until after the weekend?" Opal asked.

She really wanted to say yes. Heath had given them the perfect excuse. Neither of them needed to know it was magic. But how many more complications were there going to be? She thought about the tiger that had seemed to hit a brick wall and quickly pushed that thought from her mind. Her thoughts headed off into another equally uncomfortable direction. "Do you think our pathetic fence will keep a tiger in? Especially when it gets hungry. No, do it and do it fast. I'll catch up with Tory and Heath. You get on with the spell." Her heart sank. At least she'd had three months of having a friend. Surely that had to be better than never having had a friend for more than a couple of days, back in early primary school.

"Okay. Oh, and Eden, I'm really sorry about all this." Opal gestured vaguely. "They seemed like nice kids."

Eden started to speak. A scream echoed through the house and she froze a moment before she turned and ran towards the sound, yelling over her shoulder, "You get rid of this mess. I'll see what's happening."

In the hall, Eden paused, uncertain where to go. The sudden appearance of colourful birds flying down the stairs made up her mind. After taking the steps two at a time, she ran along the upstairs hallway. She pushed her way through vines, some of them broken from where her friends had passed. At the end of the hall, standing in the open door of one of the spare bedrooms, Heath and Tory stared at a young man slightly taller than Heath. He gripped a sword, ready to attack, and his torn and muddy clothes were of a loose flowing style. There was a cut on one cheek where blood had dried in a smear and his dark brown eyes warily watched them. His shoulder length, dark brown hair was tied at the nape of his neck with numerous strands lying around his face from where it had caught on trees and vines.

"This keeps getting better and better," Eden muttered. She had no idea what to do if he attacked. Hopefully he'd think the odds weren't good and not start swinging his sword.

"Are you one of the actors?" Tory asked. "Sorry I screamed. You startled me. I didn't expect to find anyone in this room. This set is amazing. Have you worked on many like this before?"

Eden hurried forward, her gaze continually drawn to the sword. "Can you understand us?"

"Oh, are some of the actors foreigners? What countries do they come from?" Tory asked.

"Of course I understand you. Do you think me an imbecile?" He looked at each of them, his sword still held ready.

"Well that's a relief. How'd you get inside?" Eden demanded.

"Who are you?" He brushed past Tory and Heath to stand in front of Eden. He stood at an angle so he could keep an eye on Tory and Heath as well.

"How rude. Everyone says how rude actors are," Tory exclaimed.

"I'm Eden Merrett and this is my house. Where'd you come from?"

"This is my jungle. How did it get into your house?" the boy demanded.

"Oh, god no." Eden watched as one of the tree trunks sank into the wall. "We've got to get you back to wherever you came from. This jungle's going. You need to get out of here. I don't know how this will work, but we can't have you trapped here." Eden grabbed hold of the young man's arm, but he pushed her away roughly.

"Watch it," Heath exclaimed. "You can't treat people like that."

"It's going. The jungle's going." Tory looked towards Heath. "Explain that away, Einstein. I want to go home."

Heath and the young man looked around. Heath touched one of the trees, as it seemed to be sucked into the wall. The young man stumbled backwards, his eyes widening and his mouth opening soundlessly.

"What is this? You said trap. Is this part of Melek's plan? He will not kill me like he killed my parents. Do you hear me Melek?" He raised his voice. "You are no longer family. You will not get away with this. You cannot have the crown. The people will realise if you keep killing us."

"He's crazy. They're all crazy." Tory sagged against a wall and then pulled away with a yelp as a vine slid into it.

"I have to stop this." Eden raced down the hall.

The young man chased after her. "What are you planning?"

Eden glanced over her shoulder to see Heath following, pulling Tory along the hall. Around them the jungle continued to melt into the walls. "Mum. Stop!" Eden called out as she clambered down the stairs. "You've got to stop. Now." She burst into the kitchen, the young man right behind her.

"Oh dear." Opal stopped her chant in mid sentence. "Did I call him out too?"

"I don't know. But he's from the jungle. We've got to get him back before you continue. We don't know what the spell might do to a human. It didn't matter so much with the monkeys and parrots. I mean, of course it mattered, but well, a human's different."

Eden rested her hands on her knees as she leaned forward to catch her breath.

"Yes, yes, of course you're right. Oh dear, what are we going to do with you? Where did you come from?" Opal clasped her hands together as she stared at the young man who still clutched his sword.

"Crazy. The whole world has turned crazy." Tory stood in the doorway and shook her head. "I should have listened. Everyone told me how dangerous it was to be your friend. They gave me a list a mile long. I thought it was a joke. Some of it sounded too ridiculous. And then there was that stupid story about your mother being a witch." Tory turned to her brother and grabbed the front of his shirt, shaking him. "I want to go home."

"Hold on, Tory. There's got to be a logical explanation for all this." Heath loosened her fingers and took a step away from his sister, watching her carefully. "Don't get all worked up about it."

"Worked up," Tory shrieked.

Opal gestured towards the table. "Ah, why don't we all sit down and have a nice cup of tea and a piece of cake. That is, if the snake's left the pantry." She glanced over her shoulder.

"No. I'm not eating any of the food from here. For

all I know it's got eye of newt in it or something." Tory took a step towards the back door.

Eden felt a wash of bitterness replace the anger that had been building with each word Tory had spoken. "It's too precious to waste on food. We save that for our more complex spells since it's so hard to come by. You'll only find wing of bat in the cake."

Heath chuckled and Eden glared at him.

"Food?" The young man pointed at Eden. "You will test it first."

"Do we salute too?" Eden's hands went to her hips. There was no way she was going to take orders from a kid who couldn't be much older than herself. And certainly not in her own home.

He shook his head. "No, that is for military officers. Bows and curtseys are reserved for my family."

"You've got to be kidding. Who do you think you are?" Eden demanded.

Chapter Six

"Prince Kalid of Arcassium, soon to be crowned ruler once funeral matters are complete. Then we will see how long Melek gets away with his crime."

"Ah, Prince Kalid, please take a seat. I'll see what we have for you to eat." Opal gestured towards the table. "Eden, the kettle, love." When Eden opened her mouth, Opal smiled and said, "Please." When Eden nodded, Opal disappeared into the pantry.

Eden watched the pantry door and hearing nothing out of the ordinary began to fill the kettle and put it on to boil. It seemed too ordinary a task to do with all the other craziness going on around them. Flicking the switch she faced the room, leaning against the kitchen bench. What was she meant to do with all of them?

Tory turned to her brother. "We're not going to sit around and sip tea and eat cake, are we? This can't be happening. You've got to ring Mum and Dad and tell them to get back here right away. We're going to die if we stay here any longer."

"Nice friend you are. The moment things get strange, you're ready to bail." Heath walked towards the kitchen table and sat across from Kalid who watched everyone warily. His sword leaned against the table edge and his hand stayed near the hilt.

"Strange. It went beyond strange ages ago. Now it's… oh, who knows what it is. There's no word in the English language to describe this… this… oh." Tory motioned towards the room and then threw her hands up. "I want to leave."

Eden was tempted to tell her to go ahead and leave, but as hurt as she was by Tory's attitude, she wasn't about to let her get eaten by a tiger. And not just because it would be a nightmare trying to explain it to the police.

"We aren't leaving. You're going to sit down. Let Mum and Dad stay with Grandma so they can bring her home to recover with us. And stop being as horrible as I was earlier," Heath said.

"You're not the boss of me." Tory sat at the table, sending Heath a glare. She chose the seat furthest from Kalid.

Opal soon had the table set with cake, sandwiches

and a pot of tea. She handed a wet washer to Kalid and gestured towards the cut on his cheek. "Well, I must say it certainly looks different in here without the jungle. Did anyone check to see if there's any of it left? Besides His Highness of course."

"Oh." Eden jumped up from the table. Heath followed her as she raced along the downstairs hall and stopped in front of the lounge room door.

"Are you going to open it?" Heath gestured towards the white painted timber.

Eden nodded, slowly reaching for the handle. She closed her eyes at the last moment, twisted the knob and pushed it open. She forced herself to look and nearly sagged in relief when she saw the lounge room was as crowded with trees, vines and wildlife as it had been yesterday. Remembering her mother's comments about the strange noises coming from the lounge room, Eden quickly closed the door. She turned to head back to the kitchen, but Heath stepped in front of her.

"Outside, when the tiger was after me, what happened?"

"I don't know what you mean." Eden couldn't meet Heath's gaze.

"I think you do. This is all magic, isn't it? Just like your mother said."

"What happened to everything having a logical explanation?" Eden asked.

"Magic is the logical explanation. And if that's the case, there must be some sort of logic to it. I mean, primitive culture thought nature was magic and we eventually found out it was scientific. So the same must go for magic," Heath explained. "Now, what happened with the tiger?"

"What do you think happened?" Eden glanced up at him. There was no way she was going to give him any more information. He already knew far too much.

Heath shook his head. "I don't know. One minute I could feel his breath on me and the next there was a force between us. It was like it pushed us apart. The tiger backwards and me forwards. I don't know exactly. You did some kind of magic to stop the tiger getting me."

"I can't do magic and neither can my Mum. Not really."

"Than what was that?" Heath pointed towards the lounge room.

"A mistake. Mum was trying to stop her African violet from dying and instead turned the whole house into a jungle. It's like that with all her spells. They turn out to be disasters. And me. The two times I tried to cast a spell I nearly exploded the house. I don't do magic anymore. One of us had to know when to stop. Since Mum doesn't seem to know when to give up I had to be the sensible one." Eden tried to step around Heath.

He reached for her arm, holding firmly so she couldn't move away. "You can do magic. Tory swears she didn't tell you any of that stuff you said in the rumpus room and you stopped the tiger. How did you do it?"

"They were both flukes." Eden pulled away from Heath, striding to the kitchen. She couldn't do magic. It was that simple.

"Is it still there?" Opal broke off a small piece of cake, popped it in her mouth and handed the rest of the segment to Kalid. She then did the same for Tory.

"Yes." Eden looked at each person seated at the table, her gaze stopping on her mother. "Did you taste all their food?" When her mother nodded Eden shook her head. "You're both unbelievable."

"We always have a food tester in the palace. Last year we lost two of them to poison. We have far too many enemies," Kalid said.

Eden stared at him. She was tempted to argue. But what was the point? A glance towards Tory sent a wave of weariness through her. "This is a nightmare."

She dropped into her chair. "After we've eaten you'll return to your jungle." She pointed at Kalid. Next she pointed to Opal. "Then you'll get rid of the rest of the jungle. Even Dad would have been horrified at this mess if he was still alive."

"He would not." Opal's words had a touch of anger in them. "He would have grabbed a rifle, got our swags, packed our backpacks and we would have gone on an adventure. Your father could turn everything into an adventure and see the rainbow in every storm."

Eden suddenly felt small and mean. "I know. I'm sorry, Mum." She glanced at Kalid. "But we do have to deal with this mess."

"I cannot return home yet," Kalid said.

"Why not?" Eden demanded.

"Because Melek wants to kill me." Kalid took another piece of cake from Opal.

Tory moaned and Eden glared at her. She wanted to point out that considering Tory had recently told her that she was the best friend she'd ever had, her friendship wasn't worth much since it had faltered at the first problem.

"That's all right. I'll sit here quietly and go insane. Which one of you wants to be Alice? I think I'll be the Mad Hatter. This is a tea party and as mad as you can get after all. Just don't expect me to do the song and dance bit because I've got two left feet and can't sing to save my life," Tory said airily.

"Will you shut up? I want to hear about this Melek character. If you're going to go insane we don't want to hear about it," Heath said.

"I'll pretend this is a dream. I could wake up any time I want. I just don't want to right now. And what about you Heath? What happened to your 'everything has a logical explanation' theory? Where's the logic in magic?" Tory demanded.

Heath explained what he'd told Eden in the hall earlier.

"Great, now I'm primitive." Tory glared at her brother.

Heath sighed. "If you think about it, each generation is more advanced than the last. To someone two hundred years from now, we'll probably all seem primitive compared to how advanced they are. Now can you please shut up so we can hear about Melek?" Heath turned to Kalid. "Why's he trying to kill you?"

Chapter Seven

"You would have to understand my country. In the past we have had siblings fighting against siblings over the throne as there can be only one ruler. The oldest child of the previous king or queen always succeeds them," Kalid said.

"What happens to the brothers and sisters of the king or queen?" Tory asked.

"The siblings of the ruler are the heir until the ruler has children. Then the siblings remain unmarried in case they should be called upon to be regent if the ruler dies before the children are old enough to rule. My parents died recently and once the week long funeral is over, I will be crowned king. I found myself the target of assassins and when I tried to escape through the secret passages in the palace, I overheard Melek plotting against me and admitting to killing my parents," Kalid said.

"Who is Melek?" Eden wished he'd hurry up and tell them so they could figure out the problem and get him back to his jungle. While they were inside talking, the tiger might still be outside, possibly escaping.

"The younger brother of my father. If Melek had been born first, it would have been him who became king. Instead, once I was old enough not to need a regent, should my parents die, he was not even allowed to marry since there was no one of suitable rank for him," Kalid said.

"That seems so wrong that he couldn't marry." Tory leaned forward, resting her arms on the table.

"There can be no conflict that way. While he was the heir he would have become the king if anything had happened to my father. Then after I was born, he could have become regent without owing loyalty to another country. I no longer need a regent. I am seventeen and old enough to rule in my own right. As a prince, he can only marry another direct heir. By becoming the ruler of another country, or being in direct line to rule, he must give up all claims to the throne of Arcassium," Kalid said.

"You're only seventeen?" When Kalid nodded, Heath said, "That's my age. I couldn't imagine having to rule an entire country."

"Can we focus on the problem?" Eden asked.

"It's all very fascinating," Opal said.

Eden sent her mother a look, not wanting the conversation to drift to other topics.

Tory slowly shook her head. "It's all so weird. How does Melek expect to rule by killing off your parents? Didn't you say you were now the king? Or as good as king."

"He tried to kill me too. If that had worked, he would have ruled as regent for my sister Ieesha, who is eleven. He probably would not have let her reach sixteen. That is the youngest one can be crowned. There is also my four-year-old brother Tarik. By the time he is sixteen, Melek would have earned himself a place on the council until retirement age and he would also get a higher income for having given up so many years to be regent. Rulers and officials retire by seventy. He would have given most of his years to his country, which means a very comfortable retirement," Kalid explained.

"How are you going to prove your uncle killed your parents?" Heath asked.

Kalid shrugged. "I do not know. But once I am king, I will have many guards and other resources I can use to watch Melek and find a way of proving he committed the crimes."

"You're not very upset for having just lost your parents," Tory said.

"I would not reduce my parents' lives to such insignificance by wailing and carrying on. They have gone to a better place." Kalid started to say more, but was interrupted.

"I don't-" Tory began.

"How about we don't bring religion into our discussion," Heath said. "Wars have been fought over such debates. The most important thing to do now is get Kalid back to his country."

"Prince Kalid. People have been jailed for such disrespect," Kalid said haughtily.

"Oh, get over yourself. We don't use titles around here," Tory said. Once again she interrupted what Kalid started to say. "And you're in our country."

"It is a strange country. You have great witches living in near squalor instead of in their own suite in a palace." Kalid looked around the room in distaste.

"Hey, there's nothing wrong with our place. It's been in our family for generations," Eden exclaimed.

"You have witches in your world?" Heath asked.

"Of course. Just like you do in your world." Kalid nodded towards Opal.

Heath laughed. "Probably not quite the same." He

stopped laughing suddenly. "Actually, that gives me an idea."

"What? Hurry up share it with us," Tory said.

"I take it your world is pre-technology?" Heath asked Kalid who looked confused. "You know, the lights, kettle, fridge." He pointed to each of them.

"Ah, the magical items." Kalid nodded. "We have plenty of those, but yours are very different from ours."

"A camcorder," Eden exclaimed. Seeing Heath's wary expression she protested, "I didn't read your mind. I only did it the once by accident and it's not like seeing everything in there. I was only given the information I needed at the time. Words to hurt you as much as yours had hurt me."

"Sorry," Heath muttered.

Eden nodded. She wanted to say more, but she didn't have time for an argument. They needed to deal with Kalid. Not to mention there was a tiger in the backyard. "A camcorder can zoom in further than a phone without losing picture quality. We want to make sure the images are very clear. We've got an old camcorder. Mum and Dad bought it to take all these icky videos of me doing brain dead stuff. You know, hours of me dribbling, trying to roll over, mash food in my hair. Brain dead stuff."

Opal smiled. "Sweet adorable baby stuff."

Eden rolled her eyes. "I'll get it and see if it still works. It probably needs charging though."

When Eden returned, it was to find her mother leafing through her spell book, Kalid staring at a point on the wall, Tory glaring at him and Heath grinning at the two of them. Eden sighed, not even wanting to know what had happened while she'd been gone. Instead, she placed the bulky camcorder on the kitchen table.

"That's far too big to do any undercover surveillance," Heath said.

Opal looked up at his comment. "I've got a spell in here that reduces the size of things."

"No," Heath and Eden yelled together.

"It was just a thought." Opal returned to reading the spell in front of her.

"What did you expect? It's about sixteen-years-old," Eden said. At least she was trying to find a solution.

"I've got a camcorder we can use. It's at home," Heath said.

"Just make sure Prince Kalid doesn't take his sword with him." Opal didn't look up as she continued to read.

Eden stared at her mother suspiciously. "I hope you're not planning to do another spell."

"I think I figured out where I went wrong with this one." Opal tapped her forefinger against her lip. "I believe I can heal the violet even if the counter spell takes away all the growth the spell gave it."

Eden groaned. "Mum." When would she learn that neither of them could do spells?

"You do realise it's dark outside, don't you?" Tory asked Opal.

"Of course, dear," Opal said.

"We're not meant to wander the streets after dark," Tory said.

Opal looked up again. "You won't be wandering. You have a destination in mind. Besides, you'll be safe if you go straight there and back." She looked over to Kalid. "Just leave your sword on the table."

"I did not think I could have heard you right. I cannot leave my sword behind. An unarmed prince is a dead one," Kalid said.

"In our country an armed prince is a jailed one. You're welcome to wait here with me." Opal turned back to her book.

Chapter Eight

Kalid pushed abruptly to his feet, placing his sword on the table. "There is something very wrong with your world."

"Heath," Tory hissed at her brother when he rose.

"You can stay here if you want," Heath suggested.

Tory hurriedly rose to her feet with a glance towards Opal. "I can't stay here. Who knows what might happen?"

"Make sure you use the front door. We don't know if the tiger is here or was returned along with some of the trees," Opal said.

"Oh. Unbelievable. Absolutely unbelievable. How could I have been so stupid? Of course there'd have to be some truth to all those rumours, no matter how wild they sounded," Tory said.

Eden tried not to let Tory's words hurt, but they did. She pushed away from the table, heading for the front door, Kalid at her side. She heard the siblings continue their argument behind her.

"Stop being such a baby, Tory," Heath said.

"Baby," Tory shrieked. "Don't leave me behind."

Eden heard footsteps behind her, but didn't bother to see who followed. When she reached the front door, they were both behind her. How had she been so wrong about Tory? She tugged open the door that groaned in protest. "It doesn't get used much. Dad always meant to plane a bit of timber off but there was always something more exciting to do."

"I don't think you can get much more exciting than a jungle in your house." Heath followed Eden outside.

Once everyone was out, Eden dragged the door closed. "Trust me, this is nothing. We woke up one morning to find our house on the edge of a cliff. I nearly stepped straight out the back door and over it." Eden shuddered. "Mum was trying to make a water garden. Instead we ended up on the edge of a waterfall with a hundred metre drop."

Heath grinned. "Excellent. How did you get back here?"

"I was so born to the wrong family. Do you want to swap?" Eden asked.

"No," Tory interrupted.

Eden fell silent and stared at Tory. "I always thought you were different. I guess I was wrong." She turned away and strode down the road, trying to ignore the conversation behind her.

"Nice going," Heath muttered.

"Are we to follow or do we stand here?" Kalid asked.

"Follow," Heath said.

Fifteen minutes later they were at Heath and Tory's home. Heath used his key to let them in and Eden and Tory were left to stand silently in the lounge room while Kalid explored.

"What is this big flat thing?" Kalid cautiously touched the television.

Tory strode over and turned it on. The sudden flare of colour and sound made Kalid jump back and reach for the sword that should have hung at his hip. He stared in fascination.

"Is this the jail Opal spoke of?" Kalid pointed towards the television.

Tory shook her head. "It's a TV. It shows actors ah, well acting."

"Acting where? What are these big buildings and now you are at the ocean. How does it change places so quickly?"

"Ah, well," Tory looked between Kalid and the television then glanced at Eden.

Eden hesitated. She was tempted to leave Tory to find an explanation, but she didn't think it was fair to Kalid. Not that she could give him much of an explanation. "It's magic."

Kalid nodded his head. "You have very powerful magic in your world."

Tory turned to Eden with a smile. She opened her mouth to speak, but Eden turned away from her, not interested in what she had to say. Silence greeted her action, but she couldn't be bothered to check Tory's expression. She was so over being treated like a disease. Maybe she shouldn't have let Tory become her friend. A few months of friendship wasn't worth this much pain.

Heath came back into the lounge room holding up the compact camcorder. "Got it." He looked towards Tory then Eden before his gaze returned to Tory. "What did you say this time?"

"Nothing," Tory protested.

Heath sighed. "Never mind. Let's get going." He turned off the television and, as soon as everyone was outside, locked the front door.

They strode silently along the footpath, Kalid on one side of Eden, Heath and Tory on the other. She couldn't believe it was still Friday. The weekend was going to be ridiculously long. How was she meant to survive Tory's comments until Sunday afternoon when her parents came to pick her and her brother up?

Turning a corner, Eden nearly groaned when she spotted three boys from Heath's class. They were three of the worst bullies at their school. Colin, Daniel and Patrick. How lucky could she get? She watched as Daniel nudged Colin and gestured towards them. When Patrick spoke, the three of them burst into laughter. Eden's steps slowed. Why couldn't she get a break? Was it too much to ask for something to go smoothly?

Colin stopped in front of them. "She your new girlfriend, Heath?" His companions, Daniel and Patrick laughed and Daniel elbowed Patrick.

Heath took a step to the side and tried to walk around the boys.

Eden frantically tried to think of a way to get home without harm coming to any of them. Hadn't her mother said they'd be safe if they went straight there and back? Maybe her ability to see danger coming was no longer working.

Colin stepped in front of Heath again. "What's

wrong? Aren't you going to introduce me to your mate? He looks as weird as Witchy."

Kalid took a step forward and stared Colin in the eye. "I am Prince Kalid of Arcassium. Who are you to obstruct our way?"

Heath closed his eyes momentarily and even Eden had to fight back the sinking feeling that made her want to run home and never face the world again. Why had they brought Kalid with them? She'd never hear the end of it at school on Monday. If ever.

Colin laughed as he glanced at his sidekicks. "Did you hear that? We're in His Highness' way. So what you going to do about it Prince Nobody of Nowhere."

"I give you one warning," Kalid said. "In my country this behaviour would be dealt with immediately. I only give you warning as this is not my country and rude and ill-mannered people seem to be common here. Move out of our way immediately."

Colin laughed again. His arms crossed over his chest, his stance widening, his grin firmly in place. "Make me."

It happened so fast Colin barely had time to blink before he lay on the grassed footpath. He stared up at Kalid who dusted his hands on his clothes before he stepped past him. Daniel and Patrick stood with mouths gaping as Kalid walked away. Eden followed, thinking that maybe her mother's ability to sense danger wasn't broken after all.

Heath fell in beside Kalid, dragging a stunned Tory behind him. "That was awesome, Kalid. Think you can show me how to do that?"

"You do not know the simplest of moves with which to protect yourself?" Kalid looked surprised.

Heath shook his head.

Tory tugged her hand away from her brother. "You're not going to learn how to fight. Mum and Dad already said no to martial arts."

"That wasn't martial arts," Heath said.

As they walked past the front of the Watkins' place the sound of a dog yelping, followed by a snarl, came from the backyard.

"Oh no," Eden groaned. "They'll never forgive us if their dog gets eaten." She ran towards the side gate. The simple latch seemed like a complicated procedure and it took her several attempts to open it. The sounds from the backyard grew louder.

Chapter Nine

"Eden. You can't fight a tiger." Heath grabbed her by the shoulder as she tried to enter the yard.

Eden tried to shrug him off. "Let me go." What choice did she have? Her mother's words came to mind. Straight there and back. But she had to do something. The tiger might only be after a dog right now, but what would he hunt down next?

Heath tightened his grip and handed the camcorder to Tory. "Wait here."

"I'm not stupid enough to go after a tiger with my bare hands," Tory muttered.

"I knew it was a bad idea to leave the house without my sword," Kalid said.

"You aren't all going to leave me here alone, are you," Tory demanded.

"Go tell Opal," Heath said as Eden pulled away from him.

Eden hurried into the Watkins' shadowy backyard and froze when she saw the tiger turn to see who had encroached on his territory. The small dog gave one last yelp and raced for the open gate. The tiger started to follow.

Eden picked up a stick and threw it at the tiger. With a snarl, the tiger forgot the dog and faced her. It froze for a moment before it began to stalk forward, stopping several metres from her in the pool of light cast by the feature light at the back door. The tiger's muscles bunched as it crouched. Eden's breath stopped and her heart raced. It looked like it was about to leap. Her mind frantically tried to come up with a plan. One that involved no one getting eaten.

"What's the plan?" Heath stood beside her.

"I don't know," Eden whispered. "I forgot how big it was." This was as far from straight there and back as you could get. What had she been thinking? Maybe she was crazy.

"Spread out," Kalid said from Eden's left. "Keep it confused so it does not know who to attack. Eden stay where you are. Heath and I will move."

"How?" Heath edged away from Eden.

"What we need is a net, or spears," Kalid said.

"I don't want to kill it," Eden said. "I just want to send it home."

"My home," Kalid said.

Eden shrugged and then realised the light wasn't bright enough where she stood for Kalid to clearly see her movement. "I guess."

"It will become a rug in my country. Dangerous animals that come close to towns do not last long. We value our livestock and children too much to feed them to wild beasts," Kalid said.

Eden watched as the tiger stalked towards her. "I don't think your plan is working." The tiger was little more than a patchy shadow and gleaming eyes that reflected the light from the streetlights behind Eden.

"Yah!" Kalid called out suddenly. The tiger turned his head in Kalid's direction. It stood perfectly still, as if deciding which one would make the most delicious meal.

"Eden, your mum sent Kalid's sword," Tory called from the side gate.

The tiger came to a decision, bounding towards Tory who shrieked, dropped the sword and ran.

"No," Eden screamed. Both hands went up in front of her as the tiger streaked past. "Tory!" Her left hand closed into a fist and was drawn to her body while her right pushed forward, fingers spread out. Tory flew through the air, crashed into Eden and knocked them both to the ground. The tiger was flung against the fence, collapsing in a silent heap.

Kalid collected his sword before he checked the tiger. "It still lives. Shall I finish it off?"

"No." Eden struggled to rise and catch her breath.

"Here." Heath reached her side, holding out a hand.

Eden hesitated then took it. He quickly pulled her to her feet before he turned to help his sister. She cautiously walked over to the tiger and looked down at the unconscious animal. She was tempted to reach out and touch the fur. "We've got to return it."

Kalid shook his head. "You are too soft. Lucky you do not have a country to rule or it would be overrun within a day."

"We return it," Eden said more firmly.

The dog raced into the backyard and snapped and growled at the tiger, leaping back and forth. In between his mock attacks he made high pitched excited yips.

Eden groaned. "Hurry. That's the Watkins coming home. The dog always barks like that when he hears their car." Eden leaned over the tiger and took hold of one of the legs. The warmth and softness of the fur over hard muscle and bone reminded her this was a living, dangerous animal.

"How far away are they?" Heath grabbed another leg.

"Less than a minute. Quickly." Eden tugged on the animal but it didn't move.

Kalid shook his head. "This is foolishness." He grabbed a leg.

"I'm probably going to regret this." Tory slowly came forward to help.

They half dragged, half carried the tiger through the Watkins' gate and into Eden's backyard. After a lot of struggling, they finally reached her back door.

"What happens if it wakes up?" Heath leaned against the door and ran the back of his hand across his forehead.

"Don't even think it." Eden rested her hands on her knees and wondered why she'd never bothered to lift weights before. The skill would have come in handy right now. Her arms and shoulders ached.

"We need some kind of plan." Heath stumbled as the door he leaned on opened.

"There's no need to stand outside all night." Opal stood in the doorway, a shadow with the light behind her. "Oh, you caught the tiger. Take it to the lounge room before it wakes up." She stepped inside, holding the door open wide.

Eden sighed and forced herself to grab hold of

the tiger again. It took several minutes to drag him through the house and leave him in the lounge room. As soon as the door was closed, Eden leaned against it and rubbed her arms.

"Your mother is so weird," Tory said.

"Quit it, Tory," Heath said.

"Oh come on, Heath," Tory said. "If it had been our mother she'd have freaked about us nearly being eaten alive."

"It has to be pretty major to freak Mum." Eden slid down the door she leaned against and sat on the floor. The weekend had barely begun and she couldn't stop wishing it was over. What had made her think it was a good idea to let her one and only friend stay for the weekend? Hadn't she learned anything over the years? Obviously not.

"A tiger is an ordinary occurrence." Kalid looked at each of them, a frown marring his forehead.

"Maybe where you come from, but the only tigers we see in our country are in zoos." Tory shuddered. "I thought for sure I was-" She looked at Eden. "Thank you. I-" Tory wrapped her arms around herself. "Thank you."

Eden nodded and forced herself to her feet. She didn't want gratitude. Not after all that Tory had said.

"Let's go back to the kitchen. We need to decide what to do next."

"That's it?" Tory demanded. "I nearly die and you act as if saving my life is nothing."

Eden stared at Tory. She was silent for a moment before she said softly, "We're sworn to protect life, not harm it. All life, regardless of how we feel about it. The only harm to a life that is acceptable is in the protection of another life." That wasn't the full explanation, but she really didn't want to get into all the details. It would only lead to a million questions from Heath.

"Ah, that is why you requested the tiger be returned to where it belonged." Kalid nodded. "I understand now. I apologise for my own unfortunate comment."

Tory looked away from Eden's gaze. "I'm sorry. I guess all this has thrown me. I'm sorry for everything I said."

Eden shrugged, trying to remain unaffected by Tory's words. Once she was over her brush with death, Tory would probably be back to making hurtful comments. "I'm used to it. That's why I don't normally invite people to stay. Something always happens. Come on. We need to plan our next move."

Heath grabbed Eden's arm just before she stepped

into the kitchen and pulled her out of the way so Tory and Kalid could walk past. Heath shook his head at his sister as she glanced over at them and then continued towards the table.

Chapter Ten

Eden shook his hand off her arm. "What?"

"I don't think you realise how lucky you are. Most people would love to have a life as interesting as yours. The most exciting thing that happens at our house is we order in pizza once or twice a month."

Eden shook her head and smiled wryly. "Trust me, I'd love that to be the main event of the month. Do you realise how many people have run screaming from this house because of the so called excitement?"

Heath grinned. "I'm still here, aren't I?"

Eden stared at him a moment, her expression neutral. She supposed he could easily have bailed and taken his sister with him. But he stood in front of her, a grin on his face and his dark eyes lit with excitement. "I guess you are." It seemed impossible, but he was still here and appearing to love every minute. He had to be crazy. Just as crazy as her.

"Come on. Let's go save the throne."

Eden laughed, more from relief than humour. "Sure, why not."

"What's so funny?" Tory asked when they sat at the table.

"Life," Eden said.

Tory looked at her brother who only shook his head before he turned to Kalid. "Is there somewhere we can hide and record what your uncle might say?"

"Record?" Kalid asked.

"Show him," Tory suggested.

Heath nodded and turned on the camcorder. "Introduce yourself."

Kalid looked at him in confusion.

Eden stood and moved to stand beside him. "I'm Eden Merrett, daughter of Opal and Dale Merrett descended from Arella the Wise, Guardian of the Forests."

Kalid tilted his head back and stared straight at Heath. "I am Prince Kalid of Arcassium, direct descendant of King Ismail, first ruler of Arcassium."

Heath pushed several buttons and then showed Kalid the clip.

"Amazing. You have very strong magic." Kalid touched the screen carefully. "We can do the record of Melek. Then we will prove he was the one who killed my parents and tried to kill me."

"We have to get him to admit it first," Eden said.

"Could you not use your magic to make him talk?" Kalid asked.

Opal rose to her feet and hurried to her book. "I have the perfect spell for that."

"No," they all replied together.

Eden giggled as she sat down. Crazy was obviously catching. She'd better get Kalid back to his palace before it was too late.

Opal continued to stand beside her book. "It's rather a simple spell, really. Nothing to get upset about."

"Please, Mum," Eden said. She had more than enough to deal with. There was no way she'd risk making things even worse than they already were.

Opal shrugged and instead of returning to the table, began to pour over her spell book.

Eden turned back to Kalid. "Is there somewhere we can hide to record your uncle?"

"Yes. There are many hidden passages in the palace, but they are not meant to be used by anyone other than those of the direct line of the royal family. I am sworn not to tell you," Kalid said.

"We're not from your world. We can close the

link to your world once we've dealt with your uncle. Surely that would mean us knowing your secrets wouldn't matter. There'll be no way we can tell anyone," Eden said.

Kalid nodded thoughtfully. "Under extraordinary circumstances sworn oaths can be broken. Even my siblings do not know of the passages. Or at least they do not know the secrets of them. I would think many suspect they exist."

"Now we just have to find a way to make Melek confess," Heath said.

"I will confront him. One of you must come with me and say you are a witness," Kalid suggested.

"Oh no," Tory argued. "That's too dangerous. He's a murderer. Don't even think about it, Heath."

"I will," Eden forced the words out.

Heath shook his head. "No."

Eden held up a hand to halt his words. "Listen, please. This is our mess. Mum was the one who dragged part of Kalid's world into our home. It's the responsibility of my family to sort this out."

"She can protect herself, anyway," Tory reminded her brother.

"No she can't. She doesn't know how her magic works." Heath turned to Eden. "Do you?"

She closed her eyes for a second and wished she

could answer differently. "No. But it does work when I'm in danger. Or someone else is in danger."

"Aunt Edith is very interested in the way your magic works," Opal said.

"What? You didn't. Oh, Mum. Please tell me you didn't tell her," Eden begged.

Opal shrugged. "Now she can't tell me that you have no skill. In fact, she wants us to come along to the next gathering."

"No," Eden said firmly.

"But Eden–" Opal began.

"No. Never. Not ever. Absolutely not." Eden glared at her mother.

"But you know how much I've wanted to go back to them. It was a complete misunderstanding that got us banned," Opal said.

"Gatherings?" Tory asked.

"A party for witches held four times a year," Eden said.

"Are there many witches?" Heath asked. "Are they all female or are some of them male? Is it hereditary, or can it be learned? How do you meet each other? Do–"

"Oh, quit with the questions. Let's just deal with Kalid's problem." She felt uncomfortable with the interest Heath was showing in her heritage. Magic had only ever brought her trouble.

"We have dealt with how to fix that problem," Kalid said. "We return to my country and sneak into the palace using the secret passages. Then I will confront Melek while Heath does the record."

Opal looked up from her spell book, her finger resting on a line of writing. "Do you want me to pack you some food?"

Tory gave a half laugh, half sob. "See? What did I tell you? Eden's going to face a murderer and her mother asks her if she wants to take a snack. Milk and cookies maybe? That is not natural."

Eden forced herself to grin when she saw Tory's expression. How dare she insult her mother like that? "Cookies maybe, but milk doesn't last long out of the fridge."

"What's wrong?" Opal looked between the two girls.

"She thinks you're sending me to my death," Eden said.

Opal looked from Eden to Tory. "How ridiculous. You could slip over in the bath and hit your head in just the right spot and kill yourself."

"That doesn't happen to people," Tory argued.

Opal eyed Tory. "You're a very strange girl. My

Uncle Ian was the most careful of men. Never drank, never smoked. Never ate meat. About four weeks before his twenty-eighth birthday that exact thing happened to him."

Tory's mouth dropped open. She looked over to Eden who smiled. "Your mother's joking, isn't she?" When Eden shook her head, Tory said, "It just doesn't sound possible."

"Live while you have the chance," Opal said. "Do you really want milk and cookies? Milk seems such a terrible choice. Like Eden said, it doesn't last long out of the fridge. I have fruit juice if you prefer. Or water."

Eden laughed out loud at Tory's expression. "Juice will be fine, Mum, and some water. But, I'd rather sandwiches than biscuits. They'll be more filling. I'm going upstairs to change into jeans. Wearing my school uniform to catch the bad guy doesn't seem the best fashion choice. I won't be long."

Chapter Eleven

She strode for the stairs, hurrying up them. Only a few scattered leaves remained of the jungle that had once filled the hallway. Not that it was much of an improvement. The house looked old and worn, but at least it now looked normal. If only it had looked normal that afternoon when she'd brought Tory and Heath home with her.

When Eden returned for the backpack Opal had prepared, she found that Tory and Heath had both changed from their school clothes into jeans and t-shirts.

Opal handed the backpack to Eden. "Make sure you set Great Grandma's clock before you leave."

Eden nodded and slung the backpack into place.

"Why do you need to set the clock?" Heath asked as Eden took an old wooden clock down from a shelf in the kitchen and carried it to the lounge room door.

"Stops time." Eden wound it up. "Unless of course one of us dies and then it'll start back up again. Okay, everyone go into the lounge room so I can put the clock down."

"Die? You think we're going to die?" Tory demanded.

Eden met Tory's gaze, her chin rising. "Just explaining how it works."

Heath laughed. "Come on, Tory. Let's go and check out Kalid's place."

Tory reached for the doorknob then stopped. She pulled her hand back. "What if the tiger's still there?"

"I will go first." Kalid drew his sword that once again hung in a scabbard on his belt. He looked to Tory. "If you would be good enough to push the door open and quickly step out of the way."

Tory swallowed hard and reached out with a shaking hand for the doorknob again. She gave it a quick twist and pushed on the door as she jumped behind Kalid.

"The tiger is no longer here." Kalid sheathed his sword. "I think I recognise this part of the forest." He stepped further into the lounge room, followed by Heath and Tory, who clung to her brother's arm.

Eden placed the clock on the ground, pocketed the key from it and closed the door. She joined her companions who stared at the far wall of the lounge room. None of the wall was visible. In the middle a carved stone doorway was partly obscured by the roots of a large tree. They could only see darkness through the doorway. Other trees grew closely together on each side of the carved stone, the dark green foliage making it impossible to see past them.

Heath turned on the torch Opal had given him and shone it through the doorway. Rubble lay on the ground, leaf strewn grass beyond it. "Are we going in?"

"I do know this area." Kalid stepped through the doorway. "It's a temple ruin. During the day you can see the palace just over there." He pointed out the direction.

Tory followed Kalid through the doorway to stand close to him. "It's too dark. The jungle feels like it's closing in on me." She turned to her brother who had stopped beside her, Eden on his other side. "I can't do this. You'll have to go without me. I'll wait in the kitchen with Opal."

"You won't get far past the door. Time has stopped out there," Eden warned.

Tory gulped, looking around. After one more glance towards the lounge room she turned to Eden. "I'm coming." Her voice sounded small and weak.

"Then we must hurry. We need to catch Melek in his deceits before the hour grows much later." As Kalid pushed his way through the jungle, he turned to Heath. "Turn off your magic light so we are not seen." Once the torch was out, he led the way forward until they reached the clearing the palace stood in. They remained hidden behind several large trees that ringed the clearing.

"What's wrong?" Eden stared up at the impressive stone building. It reminded her of something that was a cross between an Aztec and a Roman temple. It was a structure that towered over them in a pyramid like shape with numerous columns, entrances, balconies and steps. "What are we waiting for?"

"Hush. Those are Melek's guards. We have to find a way around them," Kalid said.

"Why not just go to another part of the palace?" Heath asked.

Kalid shook his head. "One of the entrances is here. It is the easiest one to enter."

"We need some sort of distraction. At least that's what they do in the movies," Tory said. "What?" She demanded when everyone looked at her. "Oh no, don't look at me." She held up her hands and backed away.

"There wouldn't be anything she could do

anyway," Eden said. She'd probably run at the first problem. Okay, so maybe that wasn't completely true. Tory hadn't run. She'd just continued to insult her and want to go home.

"There is. During the first six days of the funeral, anyone can ask to see the King and Queen. Most people come during the first few days, but some arrive from outlying areas even on the last day. You must tell them you came from a farm several days' travel from here and you need to return as soon as possible so you must pay your respects now. One of the guards will take you and leave the other to watch. When you have moved far enough away, but still close enough to the jungle, you must say you saw something move. Think tiger. Eyes, stripes. Remember it is too dark to see everything. Hopefully the second guard will move," Kalid said.

"And how will that help if you're all in the palace and I'm not?" Tory demanded. "You're not leaving me out here on my own. I don't want to run into the tiger."

"He would have gone to look for easier prey by now. It is rare they come this close to the palace," Kalid said.

"Oh, that's terrible," Tory said.

Kalid shrugged. "No, that is a fact of life in my

country." He glanced at the guards. "You will not be left outside. The guard will take you to see my parents who are displayed in the throne room. Hopefully the guards there are loyal and I will be able to collect you. If they are not, you will need to find a way to get behind the thrones. There is a passage entrance there."

"I can't do this." Tory clasped her hands tightly together.

"I'll do it," Heath offered.

Kalid shook his head. "No, a girl would be less suspicious. We do not want the guards to be alert."

"Then let me do it." Eden didn't want to be stuck here all night trying to get into the palace. Someone had to distract the guards.

Kalid shook his head again. "Tory has the look of my people. Her clothes are a little odd, but they will probably think she is too poor for proper clothes. You look to be a foreigner. They would keep a very close watch on you. I need you to do this for me, Tory. My siblings are in grave danger and without your help none of them will ever see sixteen years."

Tory stared up at him then slowly nodded. "I suppose I have to."

"You don't have to. I'm sure we can find another way to get past the guards," Heath said.

"I'll do it," Tory spoke a little more firmly.

"You shall be well rewarded for tonight's bravery," Kalid said.

"I only hope I live through tonight's idiocy," Tory muttered.

"You will. Mum wouldn't let us go if she could sense death about us," Eden said.

Tory frowned. "If she could sense death? Like… he's a person or something?"

Eden shook her head. "No." She tried to think how to explain the ability. "Mum mightn't be good with spells, but she can feel danger or death on a person. That's part of why she doesn't worry about me and lets me take risks most mothers wouldn't let their kids take," Eden explained. "Remember how she said we'd be safe earlier if we went straight to your house and back again?"

"But we weren't safe. The tiger nearly got us," Tory said.

"We didn't follow her advice."

"She didn't give us any advice about Arcassium," Heath said.

"But she let us go. She wouldn't have let us go if she'd sensed death's shadow close to us," Eden said.

"That doesn't make me feel any better. There's always imprisonment. Maiming. I don't know. Lots of things that could be nearly as bad as death," Tory said.

"Make up your mind, Tory. Are you going or not?" Heath asked his sister.

Chapter Twelve

Eden wished Tory would hurry up and decide and nearly cheered when she nodded her head.

"Then don't just stand here. Let's get it over with," Heath said.

With a glare for her brother, Tory stepped out of the bushes and walked towards the guards who were instantly alert. They watched as Tory spoke softly to the guards and one of them walked away with her. She stopped suddenly, shrieked and pointed into the jungle.

"Something moved in there. Something large. I saw gleaming eyes." Her voice was high pitched and she backed away, continuing to point towards the bushes.

The other guard ran to Tory. Kalid put a finger to his lips and hurried them towards the wall where the guards had stood. He reached up high, to a decorative edge that ran the length of the wall, and pressed on a button. The wall swung silently open. Equally as quiet, the three of them slipped inside and the wall closed, causing complete darkness.

Eden froze, not even willing to reach out and feel what was around her. Anything could be in here. "I can't see."

"As soon as I find the lamp we will have light," Kalid said.

"Don't worry about it." Heath switched on his torch. He shone it over the stone walls that created a narrow corridor in front of them.

"You have wonderful magic." Kalid reached out towards the torch. "May I?" He reverently handled it when Heath gave it to him, checking it over before he returned it. "Come, I will leave the lamps where they are. This is more than enough light for us."

Kalid led them through a maze of passages until Eden could not have told what direction they travelled in. Eventually he stopped. "Stay here." He moved away from them to a ladder in the wall, climbing up towards the high ceiling in this section of the passage.

Eden had noticed several of these places with high ceilings and each one had a ladder leading up the wall. Above she could see a faint glimmer of light as Kalid started to come back down the ladder. Eden waited until he was on the ground before she spoke. "What were you doing?"

"There are viewing grates at the top of each ladder. This one shows the throne room. Melek's men are in there. We will need to distract them," Kalid said.

"How?" Heath asked.

"You will stay here. Eden you must follow," Kalid said.

Did he really think she was going to follow without knowing what was happening? "Why?"

"Please, no questions. We must rescue Tory before they take her back outside. She cannot stay in the throne room all night to pay her respects." Kalid turned to Heath. "I need to use your magic light."

Heath handed Kalid the torch. "You better keep my sister safe."

Kalid nodded.

It took a lot of effort for Eden not to demand more answers. Following orders without knowing exactly what was going on just wasn't her, but Tory was in danger. As much as she was annoyed with Tory's attitude, she didn't want anything to happen to her. "Fine." She followed Kalid through the passageways, more lost than ever.

They stopped at a ladder and Kalid pointed

upwards to where a faint light illuminated the top of the ladder. "You are to climb the ladder and count to fifty."

"Okay. Then what?"

"When you reach fifty, you must use your most stern voice and demand to know what is going on. Make sure you press your mouth against the grate when you say it," Kalid said.

"Why?"

"Because the sounds do not carry very well out of these tunnels. I will return for you as soon as possible." Kalid hurried back the way they'd come, taking the light with him.

Dropping her backpack to the ground, Eden stared at the narrow rectangle of light above her. She blindly reached for the wall, feeling around until she found the ladder. Normally she didn't have anything against the dark, but this was different. Being unable to see clearly in a hidden passage, in a castle filled with the enemy, wasn't safe. Reaching the top of the ladder, she tried to get comfortable.

The cold stone pressed against her knuckles from the way she gripped the ladder. She began to wish she'd brought a jumper. No, what she really wanted was to be with the others. The eerie quiet pressed in upon her and she wished she wasn't alone. She wondered what Kalid and Heath were doing and then remembered she was supposed to count.

She hoped it had been long enough. Pressing her mouth against the grate, she took a deep breath. "What is going on here?" There was the sound of running footsteps as she battled her fear and desperately hoped the rest of the plan was working. Everyone had to be safe. Eden nearly let go of the ladder as images flooded into her mind.

Kalid speaking to Heath. "I need you to watch and tell me if the guards leave the throne room." Kalid pointed to a ladder. "Make sure your mouth is not near the grate when you speak."

Eden saw Heath at the top of a ladder next, calling down softly to Kalid, "The guards have gone."

Kalid swiftly opening a panel at the back of the throne room and beckoning Tory to hurry.

Tory in the corridor, hand pressed to her heart. "Is it possible to have a heart attack at sixteen?"

The images faded and Eden leaned her forehead against the stone wall before she slowly headed back down the ladder. Why now? She'd gone years without using magic. Now it seemed she had no control over it. Why did it have to force its way into her life now? She heard footsteps and light began to increase in the passageway. Kalid, Heath and Tory stopped in front of her. She bent to pick up her backpack, sliding her arms into the straps.

"Are you okay?" Heath shined the torch in her direction.

Eden shielded her eyes. "Point that at the floor."

"We need to get to Melek's room. Hurry." Kalid led them through more passages until he stopped at yet another ladder. He climbed up it, peered through the grate, then rejoined them on the ground. "He is not in there yet."

"So it's time to enter the lion's den," Eden said. Even though her mother hadn't seen death for them, she couldn't help thinking of Tory's earlier comments. Maiming. Now there was a cheerful thought.

"He is no lion. He would be a mangy scavenger animal. A lion symbolises royalty," Kalid said.

"Sorry," Eden muttered. It was only a saying. She wasn't exactly calling Melek a lion. She kept her protests to herself. Now didn't exactly seem like the right time to voice them.

Kalid turned to Heath. "You and your sister must both stay in here, but if something was to happen to me, this is the mechanism you push to open the door. Do not use it while anyone is in the room. The grate at the top of the ladder will be the best place for you to do your record."

Heath nodded. "Good luck."

"Thank you." Kalid opened the wall and stepped into Melek's room.

Eden gave her backpack to Heath before she followed Kalid, watching as the door silently closed. Her stomach flipped as she looked around the room. She wasn't ready for this. Why did Kalid need her to confront Melek? What about Heath? He hadn't done much. She needed to find something else to focus on before she begged to be let back into the hidden passage.

"Is all this gold and jewels normal?" Eden waved her hand to indicate the room. There seemed to be gold everywhere, including on the carved timber bed head, the heavy red velvet curtains, a trunk with gold straps around it and a stool that had a cushion embroidered with gold thread.

Kalid nodded. "Of course. We are in the palace."

She almost rolled her eyes at his comment, but didn't think he'd appreciate it. "What's the plan?"

Kalid pointed towards the heavy curtains. "You will hide behind them until it is time to step forward. You will need to listen to what I tell Melek so you know what you should say."

"How do we get away from him after he confesses?"

"That I am uncertain of," Kalid replied.

"What?" Eden couldn't believe he didn't know how they were going to escape. Was he crazy? This was what happened when you let someone lead without questioning their plan.

"Hush, someone is coming. It is time for you to hide."

Chapter Thirteen

Eden slipped behind the curtains while Kalid stepped to the side of the door so Melek wouldn't notice him straight away. She peered through the slight gap in the middle of the curtains. This was madness. Kalid was going to get her thrown into a dungeon for the rest of her life. A damp, dark dungeon with only rats for company. She shivered.

The door was flung open and a large man, with the same dark eyes and dark brown hair as Kalid, stood in the doorway.

"But my lord," a smaller man, who had followed him, protested.

Melek made a slashing motion with his hand and the man fell instantly silent. "No excuses. Find the girl and find the cause of the commotion. Deal with it immediately."

"Yes, my lord." The man bobbed his head up and

down as he backed out of the room. Melek slammed the door in his face and turned to face the room.

"Melek," Kalid said as Melek's gaze fell on him.

"What are you doing here?" Melek demanded.

"Here in the palace or here in your room?" Kalid asked.

Melek stared at him. Suddenly he smiled slightly. "Why in my room, your highness. You are of course meant to be in the palace. Is it not your home?"

Kalid ignored him and slowly crossed the room. As he walked past it, his hand trailed across the top of a table that had a gold inkwell sitting beside a quill. He left his uncle to wait for an answer. Kalid stopped abruptly and looked over at Melek. "I came to ask why you wanted me dead."

"What?" Melek spluttered. "Why never, your highness. My only wish is to serve you. How can you even think it?" His hands spread wide. "I am devastated by your accusations. Devastated."

"I have proof you killed my parents and then sent men after me," Kalid said.

"Impossible!" Melek bellowed.

"Why? Because you thought you'd covered your tracks better than that?" Kalid stood with his hands behind his back, his gaze never wavering.

"No, no, of course not. You wound me. And what

is this proof you say you have. Bring it forth and I will show you how mistaken you are," Melek said.

"I have a witch who heard you discuss the matter with your men," Kalid said.

"Impossible. Lila is… ah… well, she has been called away."

"I did not say it was Lila," Kalid said.

"No, of course you didn't, but what other witch is there at the palace?" Melek demanded.

"Step forward, Eden." Kalid didn't even glance towards the curtains. His gaze remained on his uncle.

Eden pulled the curtain aside and came forward to stand beside Kalid, hoping that somehow they'd make it out of this crazy situation. Not only alive, but with all limbs intact.

Melek glared at her. "What proof have I that she is a witch? She has the look of some foreigner."

"Do you say I lie?" Kalid asked softly, tilting his head back slightly so his gaze could meet that of his uncle's.

"No, of course not, but we have only her word of what she says she is and what she has heard." Melek gestured towards Eden.

"I have seen the powerful magic she works," Kalid said.

"Then what does she accuse me of?" Melek came

further into the room, slowly making his way to his bed as he spoke. "Well witch, what do you say I have done?"

Eden didn't know what to say. She frantically tried to think of something, relieved when Kalid spoke again.

"She claims you poisoned the king and queen with a slow acting poison so that even the food tester did not die until days later. You then sent men to hunt me down the moment I stepped outside the palace walls so I was forced to flee."

This was it? This was Kalid's plan? So far it didn't seem to be working. Melek wasn't falling for a single word. Eden glanced in the direction of the secret doorway. They would have to pass Melek to reach it. And then what? How were they meant to open it with him watching them? How were they meant to escape?

Melek stopped beside the head of his bed. "We only have her word for it."

"Then we shall have Lila truthsay the matter when she returns," Kalid said.

"No one knows where she went," Melek said.

"What have you done with Lila?" Kalid demanded.

Melek stared at Kalid for a moment before he laughed. "She is enjoying the hospitality of the dungeons until she can no longer tell anyone what she knows. Once I am the regent it will be treason for her to speak against me. Not that it will make any difference telling you." He grabbed a short sword that was beneath his pillow and held it at the ready. "One call from me and the guard at the door will be in here to deal with you. Well? What move shall you make now?" Melek sneered.

"You forget I have a powerful witch at my side." Kalid moved slightly towards the door. Eden started to move closer to him but he shook his head as he continued to move away from her. "It will be as simple as dealing with a tiger for her." His gaze momentarily met Eden's.

She hoped he meant that he wanted her to keep some distance between them. Other than that, she didn't have a clue what she could do. Dealing with the tiger had been a fluke.

"I know what witches are capable of. Healing, simple protection spells, truthsaying. Although mortal wounds are beyond even their healing powers." Melek smiled. "Shall we see how severe a wound must be before your witch cannot cure you. Then she will not be able to speak against me. I will be regent."

"She is not sworn to our country. It will make no

difference who is crowned. She can still speak the truth," Kalid said.

"Then I guess she will guide your way to the other realms tonight," Melek said.

Kalid shook his head. "You make a grave mistake lifting a sword against her. Her skills are different to those of our country."

"We will see." Melek leapt forward, his sword aimed for Kalid who drew his own sword in time to meet the blade.

"Throw the bar on the door," Kalid called to Eden as he countered each strike Melek made.

Eden raced to the door and pushed the bar of wood into the brackets on either side of the door. What was Kalid thinking? Why tell Melek she was a powerful witch? Did he think she was going to be able to save them? She couldn't do magic. She wasn't a witch. Not even her mother was a proper witch. They were going to be shoved in a dungeon for the rest of their lives.

"My lord?" A voice called from the other side of the door.

"Break it down," Melek called out to the guard.

There was a thud against the door and Eden jumped back. Behind her she could hear metal strike metal and turned to watch the fight. Again the thud sounded against the door and she didn't know where to watch. She also didn't know what to do. She had no idea how to control her abilities and had only ever used them in times of great danger. Times when she hadn't had a chance to think. At the moment she was able to do too much thinking and none of it was good.

Melek seemed to be driving Kalid closer to the door, which Eden still stood beside. She started to move away when she recalled his earlier tiger comment.

"Stay there," Kalid commanded.

Eden glanced uncertainly at the door, which now had a rhythmic thud against it. She almost giggled hysterically. Thud, clang, clang. Thud, clang, clang. The sound of the door and swords were nearly a tune. Get a grip she warned herself sternly.

"Open the door. Now," Kalid ordered.

Eden rushed to obey even though she thought it was a really bad idea.

"Guards. Halt!" Melek bellowed. But he was too late.

Chapter Fourteen

Kalid pushed Melek into the two guards, who'd been throwing themselves against the door, when they came hurtling in. They went down in a tumble of legs, arms and weapons.

"Hurry." Kalid sheathed his sword, grabbed Eden by the arm and dragged her out of the room. They ran down the corridor and turned a corner, hurrying to a door halfway along the next corridor. He pushed her inside and, with a quick check behind them, shut the door. Kalid ran to one of the walls and opened another secret panel.

"Hurry," Kalid hissed.

Hearing Melek and his guards Eden didn't argue. She had no wish to be caught. Especially since Melek thought death was the only way to keep her quiet. She didn't want to die or be shoved in a dungeon. Kalid stepped in beside her and pulled the door shut.

Eden slumped against the wall, her heart racing. Her breath came in uneven gasps from their mad dash. She thought about Tory's earlier question. Was it possible to have a heart attack at sixteen? She pressed her hand against her heart. What were the symptoms?

"We must see if Heath managed his record," Kalid said.

"He better," Eden muttered. "I'm not going through that again."

"Then we will see if we can find Lila before they shift her," Kalid said.

The last thing she wanted to do was move, but she struggled to her feet, staying close behind Kalid as he hurried through the passages. There was only the odd sprinkling of light to show their way and if it were not for the sound of Kalid's feet on the floor, Eden would have lost him. As it was, she ran into the ends of several passages before she realised she needed to turn a sharp corner. Now would have been a really good time for her magic to work properly. A ball of light would have come in handy.

"You're safe," Tory greeted them. "I thought for sure they'd get you with all the noise that was going on out there."

"Did you record?" Kalid asked Heath.

Heath nodded. "I got every word and action."

"Then we must save Lila," Kalid started to move away.

"Lila?" Tory asked.

"A witch that's been shoved in a dungeon," Eden said.

"Aren't witches liked here? I thought Kalid talked about them as if they're important," Tory said.

"Yes, but this one saw too much." Eden took her backpack from Heath, then hurried after Kalid, glad for the light from Heath's torch.

"Oh, this keeps getting better and better," Tory complained.

Kalid led them through the passages and down steps until they were on the dungeon levels. He had them wait at the bottom of one of the ladders while he climbed up and peered through a viewing grate.

"What's happening?" Tory asked when she heard Kalid groan.

He looked down towards them. "They have Lila. There are ten guards and they're taking her somewhere. I have to stop them." He hurried down the ladder.

"Are you mad?" Heath grabbed him by the shoulder.

Eden had been about to say exactly the same thing.

Kalid looked pointedly at Heath's hand. "We are in my country now. That is treason."

Heath let Kalid go. "Well don't be so stupid. One against ten aren't good odds. Can't you watch and see where they're taking her? Maybe there'll be less guards once they get her outside."

"Or more," Kalid said.

"Getting yourself killed for one person isn't going to save your family," Heath said. "Don't kings judge things by the greater good? You were the one saying Eden wouldn't make a good ruler of a country earlier because of her sentimentality. Aren't you doing the same?"

Kalid drew himself up. "I will make a great king. We will watch and see what they plan." Without waiting to see if they followed, he strode along the passages.

Tory hurried after Kalid, a glance at her brother who strode beside her. "I think you're the one who's mad, Heath. Don't touch him again. How would I explain to our parents that you were executed for treason?"

"He won't do that. We're helping him." Eden frowned. "At least I don't think he would."

"I wouldn't count on it," Tory muttered.

They followed the guards through the passages.

Kalid regularly climbed ladders and peered through the grates to see if they were going in the correct direction. Twice they had to back track and take a different passage. Eventually they could go no further.

"Can we stop now? My feet are falling off." Tory leaned against a stone wall as she stared down at her sneakers.

"A good thing we're not home." Eden bit back a smile. "Mum has a spell that'd fix that."

Tory looked at Eden for a moment and then gave her a weak smile. "They'd probably fall off."

Eden met Tory's gaze, eventually returning the smile with a half hearted one of her own. "Probably." She turned to Kalid. "What do we do now?"

"We wait for morning and my coronation," Kalid said.

Tory eyed his clothes. "Surely you aren't going to it dressed like that."

"No." Kalid looked uncertain.

"He can't go to his room for clothes, I bet someone is watching it," Heath said.

"Yes, but I cannot turn up dressed like this." Kalid turned to Eden. "I do not suppose you could use your magic to bring me my robes?"

Eden shook her head. "I wouldn't have a clue how

to go about it. What about a servant you trust? Can't you find one of them who can get your clothes for you?"

Kalid looked thoughtful for a moment and then nodded. "A very good idea."

Tory groaned. "Does that mean more walking?"

"You could wait for me here," Kalid suggested.

"No. We should all stay together," Heath said.

"Surely we aren't going to race around secret passages all night. Kalid will need some sleep before his coronation so he doesn't look like something the cat dragged in," Tory protested.

Kalid looked horrified. "I never look like a dead rat."

Eden laughed. "She didn't mean it literally. It's a saying in our world. It means you won't look your best."

Kalid looked slightly less horrified. "A king must be able to manage on little sleep when it is necessary."

"In case it hasn't escaped your notice, none of us are kings and I certainly don't manage well on little sleep," Tory complained.

"No, she gets really cranky," Heath said. "The run and take cover kind of cranky."

"How about we sort out clothes first and then find somewhere to sleep," Eden said.

"Follow me." Kalid headed down the passageway again.

Tory pushed herself away from the wall. "Anyone who says they enjoy walking is completely mad."

After another dizzying lot of passages and steps, they found themselves waiting for Kalid to look through another viewing grate. He joined them in the passage.

"You must enter quietly. I will not have the servants find out where I came into their room," Kalid warned.

He opened the secret door and they walked in silently. It was a small room with four mattresses on the floor. On every mattress slept a woman, each covered by a thin blanket. Kalid closed the door behind them and moved further into the room. He motioned to them to spread out. The only light they had to see by was Heath's torch.

"Wake up," Kalid ordered.

Chapter Fifteen

The four women were instantly awake. As soon as they saw who had called them, they threw themselves on the ground in front of him, bowing low. One woman was elderly, the other three were in their early twenties.

"My Prince," the older woman said. "We thought you were taken from us too. None have seen you for days."

"Hush," Kalid said. "I am hunted by assassins."

"Never," the old woman exclaimed.

"Do not trouble yourself about that for the moment. I have a task for each of you." Kalid motioned for them to rise.

"Anything, Prince Kalid," the old woman said and the three younger women nodded at her words.

"You must each go to my room and choose something for me to wear to the coronation tomorrow. You will all leave the garments in a different place." Kalid pointed to each woman as he spoke. "You will leave a set in the library, your set is to be left in the kitchens, you will leave clothes in my parents' old room and you," he looked at the old woman, "Shall enter my room last and leave some on my bed and take a set to the throne room, leaving them behind the thrones. Be careful who sees you and do not tell them you have seen me. Say instead you are hoping the clothes will draw me back in time for the coronation."

Each woman bowed low. The old woman chuckled. "We will tell any guards that I was woken by a dream that said we should do this to bring you back. Everyone knows how I have fretted for your return. I did not nurse first your father and then shelter you from harm as a baby to see assassins take you. I will pray to the gods to watch over you."

Kalid nodded. "Let them hear your words. Now go. The night is quickly vanishing."

Eden watched the women leave the room, sympathising with Tory. She was exhausted and wished she could go home and curl up in her own bed. Kalid was right, the night was quickly vanishing and she wouldn't mind getting some sleep before it did.

Kalid opened the secret door, beckoning them to follow him. He silently led them through the passages until he came to a ladder. He pointed towards the grate at the top. "Tory, I need you to watch for when clothes are left on my bed. If no guards are in the room you must enter by this door and take them." He showed her the catch to release the door.

"I can't stay here in the dark," Tory protested.

"The passages are not completely dark," Kalid said.

"I'll stay." Heath gave the torch to his sister.

"The dark doesn't bother me either," Eden said. Not after having faced Melek. But she kept those words to herself.

Kalid shrugged. "Then I will leave you here, Heath."

Kalid left Eden at the grate looking into the library, while he, Tory and the torch headed towards his parents' old room. Eden watched at the grate, but the guards didn't move. After awhile, the sound of footsteps drew her attention and she looked down to see Tory and Kalid. Tory clutched a set of clothes.

Eden hurried down the ladder to join them. "I hope this means we can take a break now." She gestured towards the clothes.

"Tory did well," Kalid said.

"Yes, but I don't think I'll stop shaking until a week

from today. I kept thinking every sound was a guard come to drag me off to Melek," Tory said.

Kalid took the clothes from her. "Hurry. We need to collect Heath and then we have one last place we have to visit tonight."

Eden sighed. "Even I'm getting sick of travelling through these passages." She was so tired she could have easily laid on the cold stone of the corridor and slept till morning. Maybe even afternoon.

Tory glared at Kalid's back as he started to disappear around a corner. "He mustn't be human. I'm ready to collapse."

"Don't lose him." Eden hurried after Kalid.

When they reached Heath, who hadn't managed to get any clothes, Kalid barely paused for him to climb down from the ladder.

Tory watched as Kalid disappeared around yet another corner. "If we get lost in here it'd probably take a week to find us."

"We can't be here that long. I didn't wind the clock up enough for that," Eden said.

"Oh great. What happens if we're not back before Mum and Dad are?" Tory asked.

"Don't get lost and we won't have to find out," Heath said.

They hurried after Kalid and were relieved when after about ten minutes he told them they'd arrived.

"Where are we?" Tory leaned against the passage wall, her eyes closed.

"You should enjoy this. I am the only person alive who has been in this room." Kalid opened the door and stood back so they could enter the dimly lit room.

"What the-" Heath began.

"Someone pinch me. I think I'm dreaming." Tory spun around, a grin on her face.

"I hope this doesn't mean you have to kill us now," Eden said to Kalid.

"What? No. Surely he wouldn't have to," Tory gasped.

"Of course not. You will not return to my world. It is safe to show you the main treasure room," Kalid said.

"Main?" Heath queried.

Kalid nodded. "There are six other rooms. None like this one though."

Heath slowly turned his head. "I should hope not. There's enough gold here to pave every street in our town and still have some left over. Not to mention all the jewels."

"But we won't have to die," Tory persisted.

Kalid shook his head. "I brought you here to

choose something for a reward. I owe you all a great deal for the danger you have willingly put yourselves in for me."

"Eden said her mother couldn't see any of us dying or something like that," Tory said.

"Well," Eden began.

"No. If it's bad news I don't want to hear it," Tory interrupted.

"Shut up, Tory." Heath turned to Eden. "What's the problem?"

Eden sighed. "Even my mum couldn't have seen that so many paths and choices would have been offered to us tonight. Life doesn't usually move this fast."

"What does that mean exactly?" Heath asked with exaggerated patience.

Tory covered her ears with her hands. "Doesn't matter. I'm not listening anyway." She started to hum loudly.

"Quit being a baby, Tory." With a look of disgust for his sister, Heath turned back to Eden. "Give it to us plain."

Eden smiled wryly. Plain and simple she could do. She was too tired to even think of a nicer way to word what she was about to say. "Enough has changed and enough new decisions have been made that we're probably walking on a completely different path to what we started on when we left home. Death could be a shadow hanging over any one of us."

"What? No. I'm too young to die," Tory wailed.

Heath grinned. "Thought you weren't listening."

"Didn't you hear her? She said we might die." Tory pointed an accusing finger at Eden.

Heath shrugged. "Guess you better pick out something really nice then. Make the most of having it while you can. Maybe a tiara so you can pretend you were a princess in your last hours." He waved towards the chests of gold and jewels that overflowed onto the floor.

"There are no tiaras in here." Kalid looked confused when Heath laughed.

"Humph." Tory gave her brother a daggered look before flouncing further into the room.

"We don't need any of this." Eden waved towards the treasure.

"Speak for yourself." Heath lifted a sword on an ornate belt.

Chapter Sixteen

"That is a good choice," Kalid said. "It was given to my grandfather by a foreign King wishing to make a marriage between our families."

"Was there a marriage?" Heath drew the sword from its scabbard.

Kalid shook his head. "No. His daughter did not bring enough wealth compared to what my mother brought with her."

"How awful. Imagine having to buy a husband," Tory exclaimed.

"It was not to buy a husband. The large amount of wealth she brought with her showed how much her own family valued her." Kalid moved towards a treasure chest and rummaged around inside it. He lifted out a necklace with a large red stone in a gold setting with what looked like two diamonds. "This would suit you." Kalid moved towards Tory. "Please allow me to put it on you."

Tory grumbled, but turned so Kalid could fasten the necklace. Her fingers gently touched the setting. "How on earth am I going to explain this to Mum and Dad?"

Heath grinned. "If you get killed today it won't be a problem."

"That was not funny." Tory glared at him.

Eden saw a simple gold bracelet with blue stones that marched around it in a wavy line. "This looks nice." It was something she could wear any time.

"Too little value. What you have done is worth more than that." Kalid held up an elaborate diamond necklace. "What of this?"

"I like the bracelet better." Eden slipped it onto her wrist.

"Then you shall have it." Kalid dropped the necklace into a nearby pile. "Now, there is a chest filled with silks and velvets here somewhere. We can use them to sleep on since Tory is concerned with our lack of sleep."

"Are you sure you want to waste time sleeping when this might be your last day alive?" Heath teased his sister.

"I don't know why you've always got to make a joke of things like this," Tory said.

"Because it's better to laugh than stand around shaking in your boots," Eden said.

Heath glared at Eden. "That's your opinion."

Eden stared at him for a few seconds before she smiled apologetically. She was pretty certain it had been her thought and no one else's. She turned to Tory. "I'm allowed an opinion, aren't I?" She sent a look towards Heath, who turned away. She watched as he crossed the room to help Kalid remove lengths of rich fabric from a chest.

"Who were you really speaking for?" Tory asked Eden.

Eden's gaze returned to Tory. It was several seconds before she was able to answer. "I don't read minds."

"You did earlier today… er… yesterday," Tory said.

"That was the first time I'd ever done it." Sadly it hadn't been the last. "Come on, Tory. Let's get some sleep so we're ready for Melek."

"Ready for him. I doubt it. A year's worth of sleep wouldn't have me ready to face someone like him. He can use a sword," Tory exclaimed.

Eden grinned. "So can Kalid." She paused. "Don't

borrow trouble from tomorrow. It will find you soon enough without you going looking for it."

"What's that? A witches' philosophy?" Tory demanded.

Eden's smile vanished. "No. My father always said it to me."

"Oh," Tory said softly. "Sorry."

Eden shrugged and moved away. She went to help Kalid and Heath dump the fabric into four piles for them to sleep on, dropping her backpack next to her silken bed.

Once they were all snuggled into the surprisingly soft beds, Tory pointed towards the ceiling. "How do you get the ceiling to glow like that?"

"Magic," Kalid said.

"Really?" Tory asked.

"Certainly. Just like all the magic you have in your world," Kalid said.

"But–" Tory began.

Eden interrupted. "It's magic, Tory. Go to sleep." If Tory started to explain electricity, no one would get any sleep.

"What if we oversleep," Tory asked.

"I never oversleep. My body wakes me at the correct time every day," Kalid said.

"More's the pity," Tory muttered. "I'm so tired I could sleep for a week."

"Goodnight, Tory," Heath said pointedly.

"Yeah, right. As if I'll have a good night. I'll probably have nightmares about all the ways we could die tomorrow," Tory muttered.

"You won't necessarily die," Eden said. "I just said that what Mum saw for us earlier won't be the same as what might happen to us after all the different choices we've made."

"As if that makes me feel any better," Tory said.

"Weren't you the one who was complaining they wanted sleep?" Heath asked.

"Humph." Tory rolled over, her back now to her brother.

Chapter Seventeen

"Time to rise." Kalid stood above them.

Eden looked up to see Kalid was dressed in the gold embroidered purple robe Tory had fetched for him. He was also decked out in bracelets and necklaces, his sword hanging at his side on a jewelled belt. Eden sat up. "Well don't you look very kingly."

"Don't go falling in a lake. You'd drown with all that weight." Heath rubbed his eyes as he tried to untangle himself from the fabric.

"I slept?" Tory said in surprise.

"Sweet dreams?" Heath asked.

Tory poked her tongue out at her brother. "I'm starved."

"There's the sandwiches my mum made." Eden reached for the backpack on the floor beside her.

"Do not take too long to ready yourselves." Kalid

folded one of the silk fabrics and used a knife to slide along the fold.

"What're you doing?" Eden asked.

"I will show you how to drape this material so you look more suited for a coronation. Those, what did you call them? Jeans? They will not do," Kalid said.

"I'm not changing out of my jeans." Tory took the sandwich Eden gave her.

"You will not need to. A jewelled belt and this over your clothes will be sufficient," Kalid said.

After they'd all eaten and dressed in the material Kalid had presented to each of them, Eden laughed.

"What?" Tory demanded.

Eden looked down at herself again. "We look like we belong in ancient Rome, or something, dressed like this."

"Enough talking. Do you have your record? We must confront Melek," Kalid said.

The smile Eden's words had produced quickly left Tory's face and her hand went to her stomach. "Maybe I shouldn't have eaten. I don't feel so good."

Eden knew exactly how she felt. Her hand curled into a fist as she barely kept herself from pressing her own hand to her stomach. It wouldn't be long and the entire problem would be sorted out. Hopefully with no maiming or injury and definitely no death.

"Hurry." Kalid walked to the door and opened it.

"Maybe I should wait here," Tory suggested.

Heath grabbed his sister's hand, dragging her forward. "We stick together. If something was to happen to us no one would know where to find you."

"Lila knows the secret of the passages but she can only pass it along if I am to die. Then she can only tell my sister Ieesha," Kalid said.

"That's a great help. She's been hidden away somewhere until Melek gets rid of you," Tory said.

Eden sat her backpack by the door. "Is it okay to leave my backpack here and get it later?"

"Yes. Now hurry up. Time is wasting." Kalid strode along the passage outside the treasure room.

Tory glared after Kalid. "He's so bossy."

"Come on. We don't want to get left behind," Heath said.

They hurried after Kalid, Heath's torch showing the way as they quietly followed. Eden couldn't help wondering what the meeting with Melek would be like. Could he have the guards throw them out? Or would there be too many witnesses for that? Or were all those witnesses his people?

Kalid stopped at the foot of a ladder. "Wait here. I will check what is happening in the throne room." He climbed up and watched through the grate. He turned towards them. "The throne room is full. We only wait for Melek to enter."

"How will we get in?" Eden asked. "I mean, I know we can enter by the door, but I thought you wanted it kept secret."

"We have ways around that," Kalid said. "Ah, finally. Melek has arrived. He looks very pleased with himself. We shall change that." Kalid's fingers dipped into a hole near the grate and he picked out a pebble like item. He pushed it out the grate and hurried down the ladder.

"What was that?" Heath asked Kalid.

"A distraction. Come. It should be working by now." Kalid started to open the door then stopped. "Once we enter the throne room you need to take three steps forward. Two to the left. Three steps forward, two to the right and then stop." When they nodded, he said. "Put the torch out." As soon as the torch was off Kalid opened the door and they stepped into a fog.

"I can't see anything," Tory whispered.

They moved as Kalid had directed and stood still as they waited for the room to clear. A gasp went through the crowd as the fog dispersed. Kalid stood in front of the thrones. Eden, Heath and Tory stood slightly off to his left.

"Melek." Kalid's voice rang through the room. "I accuse you of murder."

"You are overset," Melek came forward. "It is most unfortunate you have lost your parents at such an impressionable age. You have my sympathies, dear nephew."

"I have proof." Kalid turned to Heath and nodded at him. When Heath was by his side, Kalid said, "I call forward the captain of the guards, the adviser of home affairs and the steward."

Two men and a woman stepped forward to bow before Kalid.

Eden hoped Kalid knew what he was doing. How did he know these weren't Melek's people?

"I ask you to witness the image captured by the great magic these people brought with them." Kalid gestured towards Eden, Heath and Tory. "Please begin showing the record."

Heath pressed play on the camcorder, turning it so the three people Kalid had called forward could see what was recorded. Melek watched with them also. As soon as he realised what the footage was of, he drew his sword and swung at the camcorder. Heath dropped it, jumping back. The camcorder lay on the ground as Melek stood in front of Kalid, his sword pointed at his neck.

"You think you can wipe me out of existence and I will go quietly? Never. The throne should have been mine. I would have been the better king. I should have been born first. Everyone move back. I will gut him like a hare if you do not move back," Melek threatened.

Everyone stepped away from Kalid and the thrones.

"I will not go quietly. You will lead the way to the other realms," Melek warned Kalid.

"That will not help you any," Kalid said calmly.

Eden couldn't understand how Kalid could remain so calm. Did he expect her to help? She didn't have a clue what to do.

"If we die there will be no one to rule. Your sister is too young. If I cannot have the throne then let someone else take it while the country is vulnerable. A curse on your family," Melek growled.

"This is crazy," Tory exclaimed. "They're meant to be family."

"Stay out of it Tory," Heath said.

Melek looked at Eden, Heath and Tory. "And you meddling witches will follow him. The gods of death will have many more in their halls tonight."

Eden's gaze scanned the room. No one was moving. No one would help. They were going to die. She fought against the fear that made her legs threaten to give way.

"We didn't do anything," Tory said.

"You gave him the means to prove his words," Melek yelled. When a guard took a step towards them, he moved closer to Kalid and the sword at Kalid's throat caused a thin line of blood to trickle down. "Stay back. I can make it a painful or painless death. It will be the choice of those here. Anyone interferes and it will be worse for the almost king." Melek manoeuvred himself until he was behind and slightly to the right of Kalid.

"Any guards who kill you before you kill the witches shall become part of the honour guard for the next ruler," Kalid spoke loudly so all could hear.

Melek's sword tightened against Kalid's neck. "One slice and you will be finished. Any last words?"

"Do something," Tory yelled at Eden.

"I can't." Eden had no idea how to do anything. Why wasn't her magic working? She'd never been more terrified in her entire life.

Chapter Eighteen

"I can't stand this anymore. We're dead anyway." Tory pushed her brother out of the way as she drew the sword from his scabbard.

Heath tried to stop himself from falling. "What do you think you're doing?"

"Stay where you are." Melek turned his sword towards Tory who had started to run at him.

Tory froze. "What *am* I doing?" She stared at the sword in her hand before she shoved it at her brother who was close on her heels.

"Step back," Melek bellowed. "Everyone step back." The sword aimed first at Tory then Heath and then at the guards starting to inch forward. "He will die slow if anyone moves again."

Terrified, Eden watched as Melek began to bring the sword back towards Kalid. This time she felt her magic. It was like a storm rushing in on her.

She stepped forward, her mouth opening as her hand raised. "No!" The word echoed around the room as Melek was thrown back against one of the thrones, his sword clattering uselessly to the ground from the impact.

Kalid spun, drawing his sword and pointing it at Melek. "Guards. Arrest this man. He is to be tried for treason and murder."

Eden dropped to her knees, her legs no longer able to hold her up. Heath rushed to her side, quickly followed by Tory.

"Are you okay?" Heath grasped her by her arms, pulling her up.

"I've got to sit," Eden said weakly. She'd done it. She'd actually used magic. Deliberately used magic.

Melek was led past them, guards surrounding him. "I curse the lot of you." He spat in their direction. A guard hit him behind the knees and he stumbled forward before being dragged upright by a guard who held the end of a rope that bound his hands together.

"Is she well?" Kalid asked in concern as he came to stand before them.

"Need to sit," Eden whispered.

Kalid scooped Eden into his arms and strode to the throne where he gently placed her down. He smiled at her. "Try not to let the honour weaken you even further." He turned away and spoke to the captain of the guards. He pointed towards Melek's men who tried to escape as soon as they realised they were about to be arrested.

"He made a joke," Tory said in surprise.

Heath laughed. "Who would have been up to joking with everything that was happening in his life?"

"I guess," Tory said.

Eden closed her eyes, only to open them when someone grabbed her arm.

"What happened?" Tory demanded. "What's wrong with you?"

"I think I overdid things," Eden whispered.

"You're not going to die, are you?" Tory asked when Eden's eyes closed and she slumped in the throne. "Eden." She shook Eden's arm.

Eden tried to say she was fine, but the words wouldn't come. Even her body wouldn't obey. The voices sounded far away as a hand pressed against her cheek and one continued to shake her arm.

"Leave her," Kalid said. "She breathes. Give her a chance to recover."

"Oh," Tory said.

"We have a coronation to finish," Kalid said. "Off the floor, Tory."

"Still?" Tory asked in surprise.

"Of course. I must be crowned the day the last king is laid to rest. There must be no space between these events. It can bring bad luck to the people," Kalid said.

"But what about Eden?" Heath asked.

"I have sent someone to fetch a restorative for her. And here it is," Kalid said.

Eden wanted to ask what was coming. She tried once again to open her eyes. It was impossible. She tried to speak, but her mouth barely opened.

"Poor sweeting. She was magnificent. Drink this down and you will be well before you know it."

Eden recognised the voice of the old woman who had fetched clothes for Kalid. She obediently drank the sweet liquid that was tipped into her mouth. It warmed her, spreading throughout her body. Her eyes finally managed to open.

"Give it a minute sweeting and you'll be as right as rain on a drought stricken land." The old lady pushed herself to her feet.

"What was it?" Tory asked.

"Magic." The old woman shuffled away from the throne.

Kalid stepped forward and held out his hand to Eden. "Rise, Eden. I will need my throne shortly."

Eden looked up at him. She felt her energy slowly return. She smiled at Kalid and took his hand. She still felt drained, but her legs now supported her.

"I would give much to have you stay in my world," Kalid said. "Your power is amazing."

Eden shook her head. "My mother needs me at home." Those words sounded better than saying this place was far too strange for her. She'd miss her own home, her own bed and as much as the people there feared and tormented her, she'd also miss her town.

"Your mother would be welcome to join you. I would offer you your choice of positions," Kalid said.

Eden shook her head again.

"Do not decide now. Wait until you have rested and thought on it," Kalid said.

"My answer would still be the same," Eden said.

"Even if I were to offer you the position of queen?" Kalid asked.

Eden smiled. "You already told me I'd make a terrible ruler. Your Highness."

Kalid smiled sadly. "I take it there is no way I could persuade you?"

Eden shook her head. "You don't need me, Kalid. Now, don't we have a coronation to attend?"

"Yes. And you three shall sit at my right and left hands. No one shall sit closer when we attend the banquet tonight." Kalid turned back to the crowd and clapped his hands. There was instant silence. "While these three are here, you must treat them as you would me. Without them, my life would be forfeit and instead of attending my coronation I would be feasting with the dead. Let me give you Tory, Heath and Eden, the most powerful witch in the land."

The throne room rang with applause. Eden nodded her head regally, as her Aunt Edith would have done, when all she wanted was to argue that she wasn't really a witch. Tory's hands flew to her heated cheeks while Heath chuckled softly.

"Now if only I could cause such a response at school," Heath whispered to his sister.

Eden grinned. She knew exactly what Heath meant.

"Let the coronation begin," Kalid ordered.

Chapter Nineteen

Eden, Heath and Tory spent the day after the coronation with Kalid. He begged them to stay and see some of his country before they left. Heath was soon convinced when Kalid offered to have the captain of the guards teach him a few fighting moves.

While they were treated to the royal tour, some of the guards who'd been sent out to find Lila, discovered her in a cottage in the jungle. She insisted on meeting the witch who'd saved her king.

"You do not look like much." Lila eyed Eden up and down. "But looks can deceive." She stepped forward and took hold of Eden's hands. "Mmm."

"What does that mean?" Tory asked from beside Eden. It was only her and Eden with Lila, Heath was still with the captain of the guards.

Ignoring Tory, Lila said, "You have much power if you ever choose to learn how to use it properly. Do not bottle it up though. If it is not used occasionally explosions could result. Nasty things. Need to keep the levels even."

"Would they be like those explosions you told Heath about?" Tory asked Eden.

Eden shrugged, wondering what else the siblings had discussed. "I don't know."

"I think you do. You have always had the power. You have tried to push it away. It is not a bad thing. Once you learn how to control it you will have nothing more to fear from it. Use your magic. It would be a waste otherwise, as well as dangerous for you and those around you." Lila bowed to Eden as if she was royalty and then left the room.

"I wish people wouldn't bow like that," Eden said. "It makes me so uncomfortable." At school she was tormented. Here she was almost royalty. What was wrong with something in between? Something normal.

Tory rolled her eyes. "Being a queen would have been wasted on you."

Eden laughed. "We'd better find Heath. The clock won't last forever."

Tory looked sad. "I'm going to miss Kalid."

"Good." Kalid entered the room in time to hear her. "I shall miss all three of you. I was uncertain of you to start with, but you have proven yourselves to be true friends."

"Thank you," Eden said.

"Are you certain you must leave?" Kalid asked.

Eden nodded.

"Then come. We will collect Heath along the way." Kalid waved forward a servant that held Eden's backpack. "I collected your bag for you."

"Thanks." Eden took the backpack.

Kalid nodded. "Follow me."

When they found Heath, he was busy throwing the captain of the guards over his shoulder onto soft mats.

"Mum is going to freak if she ever sees you using that move," Tory said.

Heath grinned. "Nah, that one was nothing. It's the other ones that'll send her through the roof."

Kalid stepped forward and held the camcorder out to Heath. "I thank you for the use of this. All who needed to, have seen it."

Heath nodded and took the camcorder. He turned back to the captain of the guards. "Thank you."

The captain bowed to him, then turned and left them alone.

"It's time to go," Eden said.

Heath sighed. "A pity we can't stay longer. Ah well. Let's get it over with."

Kalid walked with them to the temple ruins. His personal guard followed well behind him. They stopped, each staring through the doorway into the lounge room.

"I guess this is it." Heath turned towards Kalid.

Kalid nodded. "If you were to maybe leave a little jungle behind when you send it back, I would not be displeased."

Eden smiled. "I don't know if we can manage that, but what about all the secrets we hold?"

Kalid returned her smile. "I believe the one who cannot even be tempted by becoming my queen would not be tempted by a lesser offer."

Eden laughed. "Fair enough. I'll see what we can do."

Kalid nodded. "That is all I can ask. If you manage it, I will build a palace here to protect the entrance. We cannot have just anyone walk into your world, or walk out of it."

"No, that wouldn't be good," Eden said.

"Oh, can we just go?" Tory wailed. "I hate goodbyes. I'll burst into tears soon."

Heath grimaced. "We definitely need to go. That's not a pretty sight."

"If there is ever anything I can do for you, you only have to ask," Kalid said solemnly.

"Thank you." Eden grimaced. "I think I hate goodbyes too." She threw her arms around Kalid and gave him a hug. She grinned at his expression. "We're close enough to my world that I'm sure it wasn't treason."

Kalid chuckled. "I am certain it was not."

Eden, Tory and Heath walked through the stone doorway. Each of them looked back over their shoulders one last time at Kalid standing alone, his guard well behind him. They stepped into Eden's lounge room, facing the closed door that led to the rest of the house.

"Guess we're back now," Tory said sadly.

Heath grinned. "You sound like you're sorry we're back. Aren't you the one who wasn't going?"

Tory shrugged. "I can change my mind."

"Come on." Eden opened the door. She picked up the clock and used the key to stop it. Closing the lounge room door, she stared at it for a moment. "I guess we'd better tell my mum we're back." She headed for the kitchen, Tory and Heath following her.

"There you are, love. Guess it all went well." Opal

looked up from her spell book. "Shall I send the jungle back now?"

"No!" Three voices quickly answered her.

"No need to get upset about it. I was doing fine with the spell before Kalid turned up," Opal said.

"It's not that, Mum. We just don't want to lose the jungle." Eden grinned. "It might be a nice place to go for a holiday."

"Really?" Opal looked surprised.

"We might remove some of it though. It'd be nice to be able to use the lounge room again," Eden suggested.

"Really?" Opal repeated herself.

"I could help you with it if you want," Eden said.

Opal peered at her daughter carefully. "You are Eden, aren't you? This isn't someone who's stolen your body."

"Can people do that?" Tory asked.

Eden ignored Tory. "As if I'd admit to it if I was an impersonator." She shook her head. "Really, Mum."

"You are my Eden." Opal squealed and threw her arms around her daughter. "What about the gathering?"

"Don't push it," Eden warned.

"You'll love it," Opal said.

Eden drew away from her mother. "Let's start with the jungle first."

Chapter Twenty

They all dropped exhausted into bed that night. Heath in a spare room and Tory on a mattress in Eden's room. Tory had said there was no way she could face being alone after everything that had happened. The jungle was now only a small area in the corner of the lounge room, twisted tree roots around a stone doorway. Heath had briefly returned to tell Kalid that a palace needed to be built. He'd found several guards Kalid had left behind to keep watch over the area. They had promised to deliver the message. The three of them slept late Saturday morning and Saturday afternoon found them playing pool in the rumpus room.

Eden lined up her next shot. "Will this be the last I see of you when your parents pick you up tomorrow?" The ball ricocheted off the side of the table and missed the pocket by centimetres. The three of them played their own version of Kelly pool.

"You've got to be kidding, right?" Instead of taking his shot, Heath continued to stand there. One end of his pool cue was on the floor and he leaned on the top of it.

"Well, it's not like you have a choice at the moment. You've got to wait for your parents to pick you up," Eden said.

Heath laughed. "Do I look like I'm watching the clock?"

Eden shook her head.

"If you think you're going back to visit Kalid without us, you're mad." Tory's fingers fiddled with the large red stone of her necklace.

"Does this mean you'll still want to come over sometimes?" Eden asked.

"I'll even do one better than that," Heath said.

"What?" Eden asked.

Heath grinned. "I'll say hello to you at school."

"That's only because you want to have the chance to use those new moves the captain taught you," Eden said.

Heath nodded. "There's that too."

Tory rolled her eyes. "Mum is going to freak if

she gets called up to the school because you've been fighting."

Heath shrugged, still grinning.

"If you get grounded you won't be able to visit Eden," Tory said.

"I guess I'll just have to make sure I don't get caught." Heath stepped up to the table and took his shot. He sank a ball, tried to sink another, but missed.

"Fighting at school. How are you going to avoid being caught?" Tory walked around the pool table as she checked angles. Seeing a likely one, she lined it up and took her shot. When the white ball followed hers into the pocket, she retrieved it, handing it to Eden. "I thought you needed the help." She grinned.

Eden took the ball and stared at the table. She did need the help, but she also didn't need that pointed out to her. She placed the ball on the table and eyed the angles. She felt her magic and smiled. Why not? Who would know? She hit the white ball, her magic travelling along the cue as it collided. A ball fell into the pocket, the white ball bounced off the side and hit another one into another pocket. Eden's mouth dropped open as balls fell into the pockets, one after another, until only her ball remained. The white ball came to a stop right next to it.

Eden stared at the table, unable to speak. That had been a little more than she'd planned to do.

Heath laughed. "Cheat."

"Oh. My. God." Tory stared at the table. "All of them. Perfectly. That is so unfair."

"You know," Heath stared at the table and then looked at Eden, a slight smile on his face. "There's actual competitions where you can make big money playing this game."

Eden shook her head. "No way. Don't even think about it."

Heath grinned. "How about helping me when it's cricket season then?"

Eden reluctantly smiled. Cricket season was ages away. "Maybe. Occasionally."

"Heath! That's cheating," Tory said.

"And you wouldn't do it?" Heath's grin was still firmly in place.

"I didn't say that."

Heath laughed at his sister then turned to Eden. "This is going to be a much more interesting town than I thought it'd be."

Eden's smile became a grin. "This place has always been interesting. Usually a little too interesting for most people."

Heath started to put the balls back on the pool

table. He paused, his gaze meeting Eden's. "I love interesting. Bring it on."

Free Ebook

Subscribe to Avril's newsletter to receive a free ebook. This ebook is exclusive to those on her mailing list. To find out more about this offer visit: http://www.avrilsabine.com/free-ebook/

*

We value your privacy and will not sell, rent, exchange or loan your email address to third parties. Your information is confidential and you are under no obligation to remain on the mailing list and can unsubscribe at any time.

Acknowledgements

As always, thanks to the usual crew. I'd be lost without you.

To The Reader

If you enjoyed this book, why not consider leaving a review to help other readers discover it too? Reader engagement is one of the few ways that lets an author know readers want more books in a particular series or genre. So leave a review and tell friends, not only about this book but also about other ones you've enjoyed, so you can continue to enjoy books by your favourite authors for years to come.

Dreams are meant to be lived,

Avril.

About The Author

Avril is an Australian author who lives with her family on acreage in South East Queensland. She writes mostly young adult and children's speculative fiction, but has been known to dabble in other genres. You can find more information about her at www.avrilsabine.com where you can also subscribe to her newsletter to be kept informed about new releases, current projects, blog posts and exclusive news.

Titles By Avril Sabine

Stories about strong characters and characters who discover their strengths.

SERIES

Assassins Of The Dead- Young Adult Fantasy/ Paranormal

Book 1: Dark Blade

Book 2: Dragon Touched

Book 3: Society Against Vampires

Book 4: King's Request

Dragon Blood- Young Adult Urban Fantasy (with elements of romance)

(5 book series)

Book 1: Pliethin

Book 2: Wyvern

Book 3: Surety

Book 4: Knight

Book 5: Mage

Dragon Mage- Young Adult Urban Fantasy (with elements of romance)

(Series two of Dragon Blood series)

Book 1: Promise

Dragon Blood Chronicles- Young Adult Urban Fantasy (with elements of romance)

(Companion stand alone series to Dragon Blood)

Book 1: Oath

Book 2: Betrayed

Guardians Of The Round Table- Young Adult Fantasy LitRPG

(Co-written with Storm and Rhys Petersen)

Book 1: Dexterity Fail

Book 2: Goblin Boots

Book 3: Singed Feathers

Book 4: Frog Mage

Book 5: Crystal Mine

Book 6: Cursed Harp

Rosie's Rangers- Young Adult Western Steampunk

(6 book series)

Book 1: Justice

Book 2: Vengeance

Book 3: Treachery

Book 4: Accused

Book 5: Wanted

Book 6: Corruption

Mark Of Kings- Children's Fantasy

(Upper middle grade/preteen)

(4 book series)

Book 1: The Arena

Book 2: The Island

Book 3: The Assassin

Book 4: The King

STAND ALONE SERIES

Demon Hunters- Young Adult Urban Fantasy/ Horror (with elements of romance)

Book 1: Blood Sacrifice

Book 2: Retribution

Book 3: Tainted

Book 4: Premonition

Book 5: Cursed

Book 6: Feud

Book 7: Extrication

Plea Of The Damned- Young Adult Urban Fantasy/Paranormal

(6 book series)

Book 1: Forgive Me Lucy

Book 2: Forgive Me Aiden

Book 3: Forgive Me Jena

Book 4: Forgive Me Kobe

Book 5: Forgive Me Marti

Book 6: Forgive Me Dawson

Realms Of The Fae- Young Adult Urban Fantasy (with elements of romance)

The Sword (short story in Like A Girl Anthology)

Heart Of Stone

Book 1: A Debt Owed

Book 2: Marked By The Hunt

Book 3: The Magic Collector

Book 4: An Unexpected Betrayal

Book 5: Imprisoned By Iron

Fairytales Retold (Short Stories)

Snow-White And Rose-Red

The Twelve Brothers

The Light Princess

Beauty And The Beast

Sleeping Beauty

Aschenputtel

The Golden Bird

The Frog Prince

The Death Of Koshchei The Deathless

Myths And Legends Retold (Short Stories)

Ion, Son Of Apollo

Sir Gawain And The Maid With The Narrow Sleeves

Princess Ilse, The Giant's Daughter

YOUNG ADULT NOVELS

Young Adult Fantasy (with elements of romance)

Elf Sight

Earth Bound

Young Adult Urban Fantasy

Stone Warrior (with elements of romance)

The Jungle Inside

Young Adult Contemporary (with elements of romance)

Through Your Eyes

The Ugly Stepsister

Perfect Little Princess

Young Adult Contemporary/Paranormal

Whispers In The Dark (with elements of romance and same sex relationships)

Over Too Soon (with elements of romance)

Young Adult Sci-Fi

Experiment X-One-Six (Urban Sci-Fi/Superheroes)

An Endless Dawn (Post Apocalyptic Sci-Fi)

CHILDREN'S BOOKS

Dragon Lord (Preteen/early teens) (Fantasy)

The Irish Wizard (Upper middle grade) (Urban Fantasy)

SHORT STORIES

Urban Fantasy

Eternally Late

Dealings With Joe

Glimpses (short story in That Moment When Anthology)

Contemporary

The Brat Next Door

Fantasy LitRPG

(Set in the same world as Guardians Of The Round Table Series)

Tales Of Inadon 1: The Disc (Co-written with Storm and Rhys Petersen) (short story in Game On! Anthology)

Post Apocalyptic Sci-Fi

Compulsive Directive

NONFICTION

A Year Of Weekly Writing Exercises (Creative Writing)

Cooking For Families With Allergies (Cooking) (Co-written with Storm Petersen)

Tell Me A Story, Grandma (Memoir)

NONFICTION

A Year Of Weekly Writing Exercises (Creative Writing)

Cooking For Families With Allergies (Cooking)

For the most up to date details on available titles visit:

www.avrilsabine.com/books/bibliography

Disclaimer

This is a work of fiction. Names, characters, businesses, places, events and incidents are either the products of the author's imagination or used in a fictitious manner. Any resemblance to actual persons, living or dead, or actual events is purely coincidental. The opinions expressed or beliefs held are those of the characters and should not be assumed to be the opinions or beliefs of the author.

9 781925 131277